TANGLED IN THE WEB

A QUICK BASEBALL MYSTERY #2

JEFF STANGER

 Created with Vellum

*For Simon, Holden, Walter, and Marlene.
And Gizmo.*

*Special thanks to all the members of The Indiana Writers'
Workshop: Terri Barnett, June Clair, John Clair, Steve
Heininger, Sylvia Hyde, Mark Allen Lee, Tony Perona,
Cheryl Shore, and Steve Wynalda.*

*Thanks to Dr. Kevin Ward and Pete Cava who helped with
background research.*

1
———

This story includes recreational dentistry, family feuds, and unusual tattoos (some sexy, some frightening). If I haven't scared you away yet, it also contains forgery, fraud, and fornication —all three of which took place inside a museum, of all places. There are a lot of degenerates in Cleveland. That's probably why I fit into this story so well. The city also has more than its share of spiders. And after this adventure, I can say I hate spiders.

Don't worry that I've given it all away. There's much more to this than what I just shared. And since you're still reading, I'll assume there's just enough depravity or curiosity inside you to hang with me as I unravel this tale. I like that about you. We're going to get along just fine.

In case you and I haven't bumped in to each other at some auction or collector's convention, my name is

Quick. My parents gave me the superfluous first name of Jonathan, but nobody bothers to utter it unless I'm being questioned or detained. Quick is all you really need to know. As for my occupation, I deal in baseball artifacts. There are nearly 200 years of baseball history that have been documented by American researchers. Men and women of all ages want to own a piece of that history. Whether it's a glove from the 1870s or a baseball signed by Mickey Mantle, there is a ravenous public that will pay good money for artifacts.

People pretend collecting sports memorabilia is more civilized than shooting a deer and mounting the head to the wall of your typical suburban man cave. But as you will soon see, that's not the really the case. It's my job to match the right piece to the right collector—all the while trying to avoid counterfeiters, forgers, and the other miscreants who comprise the underbelly of the collecting world. I like to think you have to get a little dirty in order to do good. Kind of like Batman, which is who I was dressed as when this story began.

It was October and I was in an office building over-looking Monument Circle in downtown Indianapolis. The space belonged to Techforce, the web-based client services provider. I was attending their Halloween party as a guest, dressed as the Caped Crusader. Chris, the friend who had invited me to the party, had disap-peared with some coworkers and left me to mingle.

I had just extracted myself from a conversation with three coders dressed as the same *Lord of the Rings* character, when I noticed a woman dressed as a roller derby blocker. She had a black and red helmet, a black shirt with a white skull, and black and red striped socks up to her knees. She was even wearing skates.

"Love your costume. You look like you could actually be in roller derby."

"That's good to know, since I *am* in roller derby," she replied.

"Really? For the Indy Tornado Chasers?"

She looked down at her shirt, which said Tornado Chasers, and then looked me in the eyes. "You're sharp. Yes," she added in a patronizing tone, "for the Tornado Chasers."

"Tell me something, do your ..."

"Boobs get black and blue after a bout?" she shook her head. "Do you know how many times I get asked that question?"

"No, I was going to ask, do your teammates cheat at Halloween too, or just you?"

"Cheat?" she asked. "How is this cheating?"

"You wear that all the time. That's not creative."

"It is, if you're trying to bring awareness to the sport." She clenched her fist, and I thought she might take a swing at me.

"Good point." I started to walk away. "Best of luck on your next bout."

She was either warming up or wasn't finished with the argument because she followed me. "Have you ever been to one?"

I ended my retreat and turned towards her. "Are you asking me out?"

She looked both ways nervously—a sure sign that there was a boyfriend around somewhere. "No," she paused. "NO. I was just ..."

I cut her off. "I'd love to come to your next bout. When is it?"

She looked both ways again and lowered her voice a little. "This Saturday, why don't you give me your name and number and I will leave you a ticket at Will Call."

"This sounds like a date," I said.

Her blue eyes glanced both ways then back to me. "It's not a date. You'll be watching me compete."

"And afterwards?"

"Depends on how the match goes," she said.

"I'll be there." I handed her my card.

"Quick Baseball Artifacts. Are you some sort of antique dealer?"

"Yes and no. I deal in relics and memorabilia from baseball's beginning in the mid 1800s to more recent items."

She pondered that for a moment, and I guess I passed the test—barely. "I suppose," she paused, "that's cool."

"It is actually. And you are?"

"Mandy, Mandy Dalton."

"And what's your roller derby name?"

I could tell by her smile she was impressed that I knew she would have a derby name. She brushed a brown curly lock that had escaped from under her helmet out of her eyes. "Mandible Crusher."

"Have you ever broken a jaw?"

"Yes, but never my own," she said and flashed a wicked smile.

"Good to know. You want me to refill our drinks?"

She glanced around nervously. "Uh, no thanks. Have a nice night." She looked both ways again. "I'll see you Saturday." Off she went and I wondered if I had blown it. Some women hear baseball artifacts and think I live in my mom's basement and sell baseball cards on eBay. Actually, things had become potentially lucrative as of late. I had recently scored the biggest find in the history of baseball collectibles. Nobody in the industry knew about it yet. It was currently locked in a safe at my showroom. I picked it up—not without risk of life and limb—in Savannah. Now, I was working on a plan to find the right buyer or the right auction. This one sale would make me a millionaire, and that's after I split half with the man who helped me find it. I could redo the showroom, or semi-retire. "So, yeah, Ms. Roller Derby," I thought out loud. "It *is* cool."

"You're off your game and you're talking to yourself." My friend Chris returned from wherever he had wandered off. He was twenty-nine, a year younger than me, and managing the customer service teams for Techforce's email clients. We met one night in college outside of a popular bar in Bloomington called Jake's. I say outside the bar, because both of us were thrown out at the same time by different bouncers for different reasons. Lying on the ground, we struck up a conversation and we're still friends today.

I turned around to face him. "What makes you say that?"

"Looks like she got away."

"She got my number," I replied.

"Wow, have things become that bad?"

"What do you mean?"

"You don't honestly think she's going to call?"

"Actually, I do. I think she's here with someone," I said. "That's why she didn't give me hers."

"Okay, that's the Quick I'm used to. Hitting on someone who already has a boyfriend."

"It's not like I knew she had a boyfriend before I approached her. And besides, she might be looking for an excuse to break it off," I reasoned.

"Come on, there are plenty of fish in the sea." He noticed a couple of ladies go by, dressed as flight attendants. "Let's go see what they are serving in first class."

My internal radar went off—and not the one that spots flight attendants. "I'll catch up with you in minute." I headed away from the party and towards a short hallway that led to a few offices and bathrooms beyond. As Chris had been talking, I could see inside an office via the reflection in a mirror in the hallway. Hanging on the office wall was a framed baseball jersey.

The door was only half open, but I could see an autographed Cubs jersey framed on the wall. Pushing the door all the way, I saw two jerseys side by side, followed by an "Oh my God" from the right. A guy dressed as Spock from *Star Trek* was making out with a sexy witch. She was livid. "Excuse us, can we have some privacy?"

"Don't mind me, I'm just getting a closer look at those." She was on the desk and he had his hands behind her back, while standing on the floor. She was leaned back not quite fully resting on the desk but showing a lot of cleavage.

"I think you've seen enough," she said.

"Not those." I pointed to the jerseys, "These."

"Seriously?" he protested.

I ignored their complaints and grabbed a chair so I could stand on it and get a closer look at the jerseys. After about twenty seconds, I jumped down and put the chair back. Surprisingly, the couple was still in the same position, staring at me in disbelief. I looked her in the eyes, then looked at him, "Sorry to break the news to you, but they're fake."

She was indignant. "They are most certainly not!" She looked down at her chest. "They're one hundred percent real."

"Not those," I said and pointed back over my shoulder. "Those!"

He let go of her and she hit her head on the desk. "Hey," he called after me as I walked back to the hallway. "I paid $1,500 for those jerseys from a top seller on eBay. I have a letter of authenticity."

"It's probably fake too." I responded without turning around. I was done at the party. Chris could have the flight attendants. Fakes and forgeries make me sick.

"MISTER QUICK?"

"Quick will do. How can I help you?" Standing before me was a pot-bellied man in a buy-one-get-one-free suit from Dudes' Depot. He wore a purple tie and an odd-looking gold lapel pin. At first glance, I thought it was an oddly shaped cross. Then I realized it was a satellite. He looked to be in his mid-fifties.

"I want you to buy a card for me. There's an auction taking place in a week and a half in Cleveland. I'll pay a flat rate, plus expenses. I'll even throw in a bonus if you come below a certain amount in the bidding."

I sized him up before answering. He was sweating a little, not from any perceived nervousness. He seemed slightly out of breath, as if the walk from wherever he had parked his car had left him winded.

"Why can't you buy it yourself?" I asked.

"I was told that if someone wanted to buy something discreetly, you were the man to talk to."

He was right. Being a buyer's agent is part of what I do. There are a wide variety of clients who will pay for this type of service. Some are new to the memorabilia world and don't want to get taken. They just need some hand holding. Others are wealthy collectors who don't want to be bothered with the pedestrian details of acquiring items. They just want to pick up the phone and demand an item be brought to them. The latter customers I actually like. There's always profit in privilege.

But at the other end of the scale, we have the obsessive compulsives and the criminals. The obsessive compulsives (or hoarders if you like) can't stop buying, so they hide deals from their wives or accountants. The criminals are just laundering money.

I wasn't sure which end of the scale he was on. He seemed like an addict pretending to be a newbie. "That's true. I just wondered why you might be in need of a buyer's agent."

"In my particular line of work, people might get the wrong idea if I bid on an expensive baseball card from the tobacco era."

Hearing the tobacco era perked me up. There would be at least one additional zero added to the sale price. "And what line of work is that?"

"I'm a preacher." I immediately had an idea of what end of the scale he was on. "But I assure you, this isn't money from my flock," he said with arms raised and palms facing towards me. "I've managed to save and invest well over the years. And being a huge fan of the sport, I wanted to get that one signature piece for my collection."

"You mentioned the tobacco era. Which card are you interested in?"

"I would like to purchase a Cy Young, T206 card. The bare-handed version." There are three variations of the Cy Young card that was produced between 1909 and 1911. One pictures him from the chest up with no hat on. One has a white uniform where you can see just a portion of his glove. In the third he's pictured in a throwing motion with one bare hand showing.

"What's it graded?" I asked.

"PSA 9," he replied.

PSA 9 meant that Professional Sports Authenticators had rated this card a nine on a ten scale. That means the quality and condition are near perfect. PSA 9s are rare for the tobacco era cards. PSA 9s of Hall of Famer Cy Young are rarer still. I asked him, "Do you realize that could fetch anywhere from sixty to ninety thousand dollars?"

"Yes, and I have it saved up. Ninety-five thousand is my high number. I'll pay you $2,000 plus expenses. For every ten percent you come under my upper limit, I'll give you one percent commission as well."

I thought about his offer for a moment. Then my mind wandered to the treasure I had hidden the day before in a small fire safe. At the time, I thought it was a wise investment. I would come to regret it later, but we'll get to that in a bit. Right then, all I could think of was getting rid of this guy and having another look at the card inside the safe. I was certain the card tucked safely away in the $49.95 safe from Walmart would fetch several million dollars. Sometimes I'm dumber than dirt.

"I appreciate the offer, Mr. ..."

He extended a sweaty hand for me to shake. "Oh, pardon me for not introducing myself. Alvin Terrell, or Pastor Terrell if you like."

I didn't like. "Alvin, it's a fine offer. But I'm going to have to pass. I'm just too busy right now."

He looked both ways. There was nobody in the shop. "Mr. Quick, is it the money? I might be able to increase the rate." He glanced around again. "You don't seem that busy to me."

"No, no it's not the money. I just have some big plans to renovate this place." I pointed to the back wall, "thinking of putting in a DJ booth and a dance floor back there," I said. "Maybe some cages and poles along the wall behind you. What do you think?"

He didn't appreciate the joke.

"The fact is, I have some projects in the works and I don't think I can leave town right at the moment."

His expression changed along with his tone. It went from gentle pleading to almost menacing. "You sure you won't reconsider?" He leaned in, "It's a simple job, and you would only be gone a couple of days."

I studied his face. He seemed ready to bring the fire and brimstone speech I had heard way too many times as a kid. "I'm sure. But thanks for the offer." He leaned back, but still had a dark look about him. "Want me to give you the names of some other dealers who might be able to help you out? I know of a guy in Cleveland who I would highly recommend. I have only dealt with him over the phone and email, but he has been reliable in the past."

"No, thanks. Are you a believer, Mr. Quick?"

"By whose definition?" I asked.

"Do you believe in God and his Son, Jesus Christ?"

"Oh sure, big fans of them both. I believe the disciples could have taken the pennant that year if they hadn't lost their star pitcher."

"Come again?"

"Your ace starter gets arrested, tried, convicted, and executed in one weekend—it's tough to recover from that. Although I have to give him credit, he didn't stay on the DL that long—three days!"

"Mock the Lord at your own peril."

"I happen to believe God has a sense of humor."

"Well, I've been a Church of the Galilean preacher for many years and I can tell you with 100 percent certainty that God's sense of humor is never mentioned in the Bible."

A Galilean. Well, that explains it. Guess that's why I could tell he was nearing fire and brimstone mode a moment ago. I spent the first eighteen years of my life under the tyranny of the Galileans. I escaped to college and never looked back. I believed in God, just not their brand. And I wasn't all that interested in sampling any others for that matter. Regardless, I knew enough not to get into a long debate with this guy.

"He never mentions baseball either, but you seem to get a lot of joy out of it. Enough to buy a baseball card worth tens of thousands of dollars. At any rate, I don't want to argue with you. I can't do the job for you next week. Let's leave it at that."

"I'm disappointed to hear that, Mr. Quick." He reached up and fidgeted with the odd lapel pin for a second. Then he laid his card on the counter and added, "But I have a feeling you will see the light."

He said goodbye and left. The store was empty, and nobody seemed to be approaching from the outside. My only employee, Kevin, wouldn't be in until later. He's a grad student in his mid-twenties. I've lost track of the majors he's had. They usually change when he is in danger of graduating.

Kneeling behind the counter, I removed a 14-by-30 vent cover from the wall. Behind the cover wasn't duct-work but a clever hiding place. From the office behind, the space was drywalled and looked like a hidden support beam. I reached into the opening and pulled out the $49.95 safe I had recently purchased. It was about the size of a small briefcase, but thicker and heavier. Fumbling in my pocket, I searched for the key to unlock it.

Once I had it, I slid the key in and opened the safe. Inside was a single item in a protective plastic cover. It contained a T206 tobacco card, just like the preacher was looking for. However, this one was much more valuable. It was a signed Honus Wagner. The only one known to exist. The holy grail of all baseball cards. All I had to do was sell it, and I could put an end to dealing with guys like the one who had just left.

However, I was conflicted. I'm a collector, too. So, for past two months, I had been stalling on putting it up for auction. This card could set me up for life. Plus, I had made an agreement to split the proceeds with the ex-ballplayer who helped me find it. But it was also a once in a lifetime find. Only one other living person besides the old ballplayer knew it even existed, and he was in jail. I stared at it for a while and considered again whether to sell it or keep it.

Why was this so hard? The T206 tobacco cards are the most sought-after baseball cards around. They were produced from 1909 to 1911 by the American Tobacco Company and inserted into cigarette and loose tobacco packs covering 16 different brands. They are incredibly rare and valuable for a variety of reasons. First, there were a lot of Hall of Fame baseball players included in the set. Second, card collecting wasn't an organized hobby back then, so most people tossed them aside. Few have survived the past 100 years. Some are more valuable based on the brand name that is on the back. And of course, the most valuable one is that of Hall of Fame baseball player Honus Wagner. Legend has it he didn't want his name associated with a product that might encourage kids to smoke, so he protested its release. Only fifty to 200 were thought to have been sold and of those fewer than forty are known to survive. A

T206 in any condition can go for tens of thousands of dollars. And one in good condition will fetch several million dollars. But don't go running to grandma's attic just yet. You might just find one of these. Before you do, I want you to know all the trouble it caused me. Then you can decide if it's better to let it stay hidden.

Every day since I had returned from Savannah with that card, I had pulled it out of the safe and dreamed of the possibilities. I was Gollum, obsessed with the one true Ring. It was my Precious.

Finally, I came out of the daydream and slid it back into the safe. I closed the lid, turned the key, and put the safe back into its hiding place. With the vent cover back in place, I returned the key to my pocket. I might as well have thrown it away. That was the last time I would ever use it.

2

"Do you like Shackled Fudge?"

I didn't recognize the woman's voice on the other end of the phone. "Who is this?"

"It's Mandy, from the Halloween party?"

"Were you the blonde Wonder Woman or the brunette?"

She seemed upset. "How many women did you give your number to at that party?"

"Just one, the roller derby chick. Is that you?"

"That's me. Although I'm starting to have my doubts about this."

"Don't doubt, don't doubt," I pleaded. "I promise you were the only one I gave a card to."

"Okay, well I wanted to see if you would like to go see Shackled Fudge. They're playing at the Vogue tonight."

"Sure, I can clear my schedule." I didn't have

anything planned. "Want to meet at Moe & Johnny's bar for dinner beforehand?"

"No, just meet me at the Vogue. I'll have your ticket."

When I got to the show, there was a line about twenty deep waiting to get in. The Vogue is a landmark concert venue in Indianapolis. It opened as a movie theatre in the 1930s and was converted into a nightclub in the late 1970s. Tables and chairs line the walls while the bar and dance floor fill the space where the old theatre seats were located. The stage is large enough to have nationally known acts, but small enough to make performances feel intimate.

The doors were open, so I got in line and texted Mandy that I was there. Just when I got to the front, she seemed to appear out of nowhere. She nervously said hello while carefully looking around as if she was worried about being followed. I pretended not to notice.

I did notice she wore a black skirt with black Converse All Stars. On top, she wore a red Aztec Freddy Brewery long sleeve t-shirt.

Mandy scouted for a place to watch the show while I bought a couple of beers. I found her to the right of the stage, about five rows of humanity back from the front. We managed to finish about half our beers before the lights went out. All around us people starting chanting, "Fudge, fudge, fudge."

A screen dropped down and the image of an oven appeared. The crowd shouted even louder. The timer on the oven was counting down from 30 seconds. As it did, you could see the shadows of musicians taking their places on stage.

When the timer got to zero, the oven door popped open and out came a hot tray of brownies. The first notes from an electric guitar could be heard, the video disappeared, and the stage lights cloaked the band in blue.

The crowd went crazy as Shackled Fudge played their hit *Lick the Mixing Bowl*. Mandy squeezed my hand and sang along, word for word. Song after song, she knew all the words. It was a fun show with a fun crowd, at least the parts I can remember.

Midway through the show, she pulled me in tight and kissed me. After a while, I realized we had kissed through an entire song. Pretty soon we were tucked into a corner of the bar and making out like teenagers. We did manage to stop for the finale and the encore—this was Shackled Fudge after all.

If you've never been to one of their shows, make sure to stay to the end. That's when the fudge becomes unshackled, so to speak. The band is known to pelt the audience with brownies (often of the fudge/pot variety), fudge chunks, hot fudge, and whatever else they feel like slinging onto the crowd.

Sure enough, as they were playing an acoustic version of their hit, "She Dumped Me at Jockamo's," the bass player started shooting warm brownies out of one of those T-shirt cannons you see at sports arenas. I got hit in the cheek with a piece of chocolate goodness.

Before I could react, Mandy licked it off my face. "My God, those brownies are good!"

"Wait here," I replied. "I'll see if I can get hit in a few more places."

I tried desperately to get hit by the brownie cannon again, but I failed.

When the show was over, Mandy told me she had a lovely time and hoped to see me again soon. I'm thinking, why on earth would you want this to end? "Want to get a drink?"

"No, I'm good. I've got an early day tomorrow."

"Can I walk you to your car?"

"I didn't drive. I only live a few blocks from here."

"Then I'll walk you home." I thought I'd found an opening.

"That's sweet, but I can take care of myself." True. She was in better shape than me, athletic and at least an inch taller. She continued, "Besides, I don't want to rush into this too fast."

Too fast, I wondered to myself. Your tongue was in my mouth just five minutes ago. However, I wasn't going to push it. "No problem," I said. "Thanks for the ticket."

We walked out together at least, then she said good-bye, looked both ways and scurried off.

I can be dense at times, but I do know when someone is hiding something. I was pretty sure she had a boyfriend or heaven forbid a husband back at home. I figured this was probably a bad idea and resolved to let this be our only date.

Until the next day when she did the same thing. Invites me out, shows up just in time, makes out like crazy, then hightails it out the door. I was being used, I know. At first, I didn't question it because the kissing was good. Really, really good. I suppose I figured that other activities might be even better. But after two awkward endings, her nervousness made me fear there might be somebody dangerous on the other side of this. So, when Saturday rolled around, I decided to break it off.

I arrived early at the Exposition Hall of the Indiana State Fairgrounds. My plan was to end it before the bout started. This would give me time to escape and she could burn off any hostility towards me while she competed. A junior roller derby match was going on when I arrived. They were junior in experience, not in age. A lively crowd of about two hundred people was cheering them on.

I texted Mandy, and she asked me to meet her in a hallway that was off limits to the general public. I could see her waiting with a security guard in front of a black curtain that hid the rest of the hallway from view. At her request, the security guard let me pass and we walked behind the curtain.

As soon as we were about ten feet past the curtain, Mandy shoved me against the cold concrete wall, pinned my arms in place and stuck her tongue in my mouth. I've been with some aggressive women in my day, but this felt like being sacked by an entire defensive line. After exploring every corner of my mouth, she stepped back and said, "We have to talk."

Wait, wasn't that why I had come to see her before her bout? And I know what "we have to talk" means. I just wasn't used to it coming out of someone else's mouth.

She paused with a strange look on her face. I figured I would let her speak first. Instead she pinned me against the wall again and kissed me. "No really," she pulled away. "We have got to talk." I could tell she was conflicted. She pushed me against the wall for another kiss. I could *feel* she was conflicted.

I waited until the silence was uncomfortable. I offered, "Still trying to sort it out?"

"This isn't easy for me to say. I can't seem to come up with the right words."

"Maybe you should keep kissing me until you find them."

"Good idea." She pinned me again. As much as I was enjoying making out with her, my head was taking a beating on the arena wall.

"Okay, okay. I've got this." She looked me in the eyes. "I'm bi-curious."

Suddenly I was reconsidering the breakup. "Are you saying you're interested in experimentation?"

"Yes."

Have you ever had things seem to fall into your lap like this? I thought I had won the naughty lottery. "That's okay." I didn't want to sound too excited. "I'm fine with that. Is there a particular woman you're interested in or just the overall concept?"

She looked at me like I was an idiot. "No, I'm curious about men."

"Oh," I said. Not an "I get it" oh. It was a fill-in-the uncomfortable-silence-while-I-ponder-what-was-just-said oh. "I don't think I get it, maybe you should kiss me again."

Miraculously that worked. She pinned me against the wall and gave me an amorous what-for. She backed off again and that's when it hit me. Literally and figuratively. Inside my thick skull, it hit me that she was a lesbian who was bi-curious, and I was the curiosity. Outside my thick skull, it hit me with a fist. "It" being her teammate and lover, Terminator Tanya. She was larger than an NFL tight end and twice as mean.

Terminator Tanya had spiked red hair. Not natural red, mind you. I mean fire engine red. I can't even imagine what chemical process would produce hair that color. She wore a sleeveless black Tornado Chasers shirt and black shiny shorts with black and red striped tights underneath. On her right bicep, she had a tattoo of the robot skull from the movie *Terminator.* On her left bicep, she had the silver shape from *Terminator* 2. I can only imagine where she had the villains from *Terminators* 3 and 4.

She hit me several times before I even had the sense to cover my face. After knocking me to the ground, she said, "Get up, bitch. Mandible Crusher belongs to me."

I looked up. "I don't want to fight you. I had no idea she was ..."

She kicked me, then ordered me to get up and fight. I struggled to my feet and held out my arms. I repeated, "I don't want to fight you."

"Why not?"

"Because I had no idea you two were together." I looked at Mandy, "Tell her."

She shrugged and looked at Tanya. "I was curious. Can't a girl be curious?"

Tanya punched me. "Come on, are we going to do this or what?"

"I'm not going to fight you."

"Why not?"

Sometimes my stupidity knows no bounds. There was only one thing I could have said that would guarantee that Terminator Tanya would kick my ass, and I was dumb enough to say it. "Because you're a girl."

Flames shot out of her eyes. She let out a cry that to this day haunts the children of anyone in a mile-wide radius of the venue that night. She pummeled me into unconsciousness. When I awoke, the team trainer had smelling salts under my nose. Kneeling on the other side of me, a skater from the junior team was holding a bloody tooth and smiling. I assumed the tooth was mine. I moved my tongue around my mouth and was horrified. I expected to feel the absence of a front tooth. Instead, I was missing one from the back—a molar. She had knocked out one of my back teeth! I couldn't imagine how bloodied and bruised my face must be. No wonder I blacked out.

"I saved your tooth," the junior skater said. She was all smiles, as if she had done the most philanthropic thing in the world by holding on to my tooth while I came back to the world.

The trainer informed me, "You'll need to go to the emergency room."

I didn't want to go, but I was in too much pain to argue. "Okay", I said.

"Do you have any idea how this happened?" he asked.

Terminator Tanya was standing behind them in a crowd of onlookers. Glaring. She even made a fist and punched her other hand. "Nope, no idea at all," I answered. She slowly nodded.

"Want me to come to the hospital with you?" asked the junior skater. "I could carry your tooth."

"You can just tuck it into my shirt pocket, thanks." I rested my head back on the ground.

"It's gone," she said.

I leaned back up to look at my torso. Sure enough, the pocket had been ripped off my shirt. I was also missing part of my pant leg. I'm sure I looked as if I had been mauled by dogs. I looked up at the girl holding my tooth and she smiled. Then I blacked out again.

WHEN I AWOKE, annoyingly cheerful skater girl was sitting by my side. There were a variety of plugs and wires coming out of me. "They're going to keep you overnight," she said.

"Anything serious?"

"They said you had a slight concussion."

"How long have I been out?"

"It's midnight."

"You should go home and get some rest. You really didn't have to stay with me," I told her.

"I promised you I would carry your tooth." She held it up like a prize.

"That's very kind of you. Shouldn't that be in milk or something?"

"No, the doctor said the way it was torn out, a dentist would probably just replace it with an implant."

"But you're still holding it?" I asked.

"Uh huh." She said it like it was the most logical thing in the world for her to be sitting here next to me holding my tooth. I was too foggy to figure this out. But here I was in the hospital, having started the day planning to break up with a derby girl, subsequently being severely beaten by a second one, and finally winding up in the hospital with what might very well be a chemically unbalanced third. This was too much.

"I think you should go home now. We'll talk when I get out."

"Don't be silly. I'll be back first thing in the morning.

Unless," she paused and looked me up and down, "you want me to crawl in bed with you."

For a millisecond, I pondered this new development. Temptation is always jumping out of the strangest places. It simply isn't fair to dangle iniquity in front of me when I'm in such a compromised mental state. But the pain in my mouth returned in time to bring me back to reason and righteousness. "That's a sweet and wonderful offer, but I better get my rest. By the way, what's your name?"

"I'm Simone."

"Nice to meet you. My name's Quick."

"I know, I went through your wallet," she replied.

I tried to process what that meant, then decided it was too much for me to sort through. "I think I better get some sleep now."

"Okay, sweet dreams." She leaned over and kissed my cheek. As she walked out, she stopped and whirled around. "What do you want me to do with your tooth?"

"Leave it on the nightstand if you don't mind. I might want it someday."

"I knew it. Now, aren't you glad I held onto it?"

She placed the tooth on the table beside me and gave me one last kiss on the cheek. "Goodnight." My rest lasted a moment if that. A nurse entered and started mumbling in front of my chart. Next, she mumbled in front of the big screen with all the vital signs. Then she mumbled at my IV. Finally, she said something I could hear. "You're looking better, Mr. Quick."

"Better than what?"

"Then the bloody pulp you looked like when you came in."

"Oh, I clean up pretty well."

"Rumor has it you had your ass kicked by a girl."

How did she know that? I didn't even tell the police. She grinned at my bewilderment. I tried to get out a question and she just chuckled and shook her head. Then she placed her foot on the side of my bed and slowly pulled up the pant leg on her scrubs. Halfway up the calf she had a Tornado Chasers tattoo. She shook her head at me, pulled her pant leg down, and laughed as she walked out the door.

3

The next day the doctors decided my brain wasn't damaged to the point of keeping me. As I was filling out the release paperwork, a nurse asked me how I planned to get home.

"I'll be taking care of him," came a voice from the hall. Simone was back. "And how are you this morning?"

I looked at the nurse. "Can I stay?"

She looked at Simone and then back at me. "No, I don't think so. Besides, you seem to be in great hands."

"I detect sarcasm." I flipped through the pages of hospital legalese on the release forms. "Am I paying extra for that? I can't seem to find it in here."

She took the papers from me and returned them to her clipboard. "For someone like you," she looked back at the girl, "it's free of charge."

Someone like me? What the heck did that mean? It's not like I wanted a ride home from this squealing twenty-something woman. I just wanted quiet and sleep.

Simone walked me out to her car and told me she wasn't taking me home. She thought I should see the dentist first. Okay, she was annoying, but she was thinking more clearly than I was. I needed to get to the dentist before the drugs had worn off, I decided. I pulled out my phone. "Let me see if I can get an appointment with my dentist."

"Dr. Walsh, right?"

How did she know that? "Yes, that's him."

"He'll see you at 1:30. We've got 20 minutes to get there."

"You made me an appointment? How did you know he was my dentist?"

"Because I stopped by your house, silly."

Strange music should have been playing in the background at that point. "You went to my house? Why? And how did you get in?"

"I picked up some clothes and a toothbrush so you could stay with me until you get better," she said.

"Stay with you?"

"Yes, who else is going to take care of you? Mandy isn't."

"But I don't need taking care of. And you never said how you got into my house?"

"I took your keys from the hospital. Then I got an Uber back to the Fairgrounds, picked up your car, ran by your house, then drove it to my place."

As she said this, none of it seemed odd or unusual to her. It sure as hell did to me, but not to her. I didn't know what to make of it.

"Look, I really think I can take care of myself. I appreciate all you've done, but I think I'll be okay."

"I want to do it. Besides, I don't think you have any idea how bad it's going to hurt when all the pain meds wear off."

I thought about it. She was probably right, and I didn't really have anyone to take care of me. But Simone had all the ingredients of the creepy stalker future ex-girlfriend.

I should have said no. Instead, I said, "I'm not sure."

"Why don't you wait until after you've been to the dentist to decide?" she replied.

I MUST HAVE DOZED off again or been under the influence of the pain meds. I don't remember arriving at the dentist, checking in, or filling out any paperwork. The only thing I remember from my time in the waiting room was a mom chasing her toddler son around. He had managed to get his hand down into a fish tank and wrangle out a goldfish. Then he raced around the room with it high above his head, shouting something about Nemo. I may have dreamt this. It's hard to tell.

A hygienist called my name and I had to convince Simone I could go in by myself. I followed her to the examination room and waited for the dentist.

"Quick, how are you?"

"I've been better."

"So I hear." He leaned in close and lowered his voice. "Say, you haven't come across any Larry Doby items lately, have you?"

Being an Indians fan, he always asked me for a tip on any Cleveland merchandise I might come across. Larry Doby was the first African American to play in the American League. Though Jackie Robinson rightfully is celebrated as the first black player in the Major Leagues, Doby's first season was no less a struggle for equality and acceptance.

"Nothing lately, but I'll keep my eyes open." He seemed disappointed. "What's your budget these days, in case I do come across something?"

"I'm good for something up to $1,000. But it has to be vintage," he added.

"I will find you something."

He added, "We had dinner with one of my college buddies last week. He's a real Cleveland fan and he has deep pockets. Owns a chain of dental care outlets in Ohio. He once bought a Nap Lajoie baseball card for $140,000. Would I get a commission if you found something for him?"

"I think we could work something out," I answered. I find it best to be accommodating to dentists and law enforcement.

"Okay, let's have a look at the damage."

He spent a few minutes studying the hole in my lower left jaw. There were several points when he uttered a "hmm." Finally, he gave me his diagnosis.

"We have three choices." I knew I wasn't going to like any of them. "We can let things heal up and leave the tooth missing. We can do a bridge, but that would require us to put crowns on the tooth in front and the one in back. Then attached to both would be the replacement tooth."

"And the third option?"

"We can do an implant." I glanced at the dental assistant and then back to the doctor. He continued. "That would require putting a post into the bone. That heals and sets for about twelve to eighteen weeks. Then we put an abutment on top of that. Once that is in, we do an impression and send it to the lab. Two weeks later, you come in and we put the new crown in place."

"So, I'm looking at about five months without a tooth?"

"That's correct."

"Alright, I suppose the implant is going to be the best option. Let's do it."

"We'll want to give that some time to heal and schedule an appointment with an oral surgeon. In the meantime, we need to stitch up a couple of places that look problematic to me. When we finish, I'll prescribe some antibiotics to help keep that from getting infected and some pain killers."

"Can you knock me out?"

"Looks like somebody already did." He chuckled. I groaned. "I can't put you all the way under, but I'll make sure you don't feel anything. I see you have a ride home." I glanced over to see that Simone had not been able to wait any longer. She saw the doctor's acknowledgment as an opportunity to get involved. "I'll take good care of him, don't you worry. By the way, do you need this tooth?"

He looked at the tooth and then at me. "Yours?"

"The tooth or the girl?"

"Both."

She answered for me while holding the tooth in the plastic bag and shaking it. "Of course, we're both his."

He looked at me and I begged him with my eyes. He seemed to understand my plight. "Let's get you sedated," he said.

Although they didn't put me under, I really don't remember much of the next hour or so. I was numb and still woozy and in pain from the beating. We went to a pharmacy to get the meds the dentist prescribed and then Simone took me to her place. I fell asleep on her couch and didn't wake up until 6:30 the next morning.

Simone was still sleeping, so I wrote her a thank you

note, found the stack of clothes she had packed for me, and let myself out. An hour later, she called me. "Where are you?"

"I'm at home."

"I'm coming over."

"No, really I'm fine. Let me get some rest and we can talk later today."

"Talk, what do we need to talk about? Are you breaking up with me?"

"Breaking up with you? Are we together?" I thought for a moment. Maybe I do have a concussion. Was I dating this girl, too—before I got beat up? I wouldn't have put it past myself—dating two girls at once—but choosing this one seemed a stretch from my normal routine.

"You'll regret this."

"We just met. We hardly know each other!"

"How can you say that after I cared for you and saved your tooth?"

"Look, I'm not feeling well. I'm not thinking clearly. How about I get some rest and we can talk about it later?"

"Fine, get some rest and I'll be there for lunch."

I was too tired to argue.

"Okay."

Sure enough, my doorbell rang at noon. "I brought soup," she announced. "I figured that would be easier for you to eat."

"Thank you."

"See, you need me. You just don't want to admit it." I didn't answer. She made small talk for a while, but the only thing I remember was she worked at a bookstore and her shift was from 2-10 p.m. that day. "I can call in sick if you need me to stay."

"I will be fine," I said.

"I'm glad to see you're feeling better," she said. "And it's good to know you're not breaking up with me."

I put down my soup. "Look, all I can remember is waking up from a beating and you were by my side. Please don't take this the wrong way. It could be the head injury. Were we dating before I got beat up at the Fairgrounds?"

"No."

"So, the first time you saw me was then?"

"No, I saw you on dates with Mandy. Mandy's my mentor."

"Oh, then you knew she had a girlfriend."

"Of course. I'm the one who told Terminator Tanya that Mandy was cheating."

"Why did you do that? She beat the hell out of me!"

"I'm really sorry about that, but I knew Mandy wouldn't let me have you unless you broke up. Once Tanya put the beatdown on you, I asked Mandy if I could have you and she said yes. See! It all worked out."

"No! It did not work out. I don't have a tooth! And we're not together!"

"We're together now."

"No, I want you to leave. Now!"

She stood up and threw the soup at me. "After what I sacrificed, I can't believe you would be so ungrateful."

"You sacrificed? I lost a tooth, lady!"

"How dare you call me 'lady?' "

"Just go."

"You're going to regret this." She glared at me while moving backwards towards the door. She stopped and checked her purse for her keys. "I will make you pay," her voice dropped down a few octaves. Now it was an evil whisper. "And I'm keeping your tooth!"

She slammed the door on her way out and I collapsed back into the couch. I stared at the ceiling for a while. I have to re-evaluate my life, I thought. I need to hang out with different people. When I sell that card, I'm changing everything. I drifted off thinking about the possibilities of three, maybe four million dollars.

When I awoke, my cell phone was ringing. "Hello."

"Mr. Quick? Are you the owner of Quick's Baseball Artifacts?

I didn't have the energy for my usual snarky reply. And something in his town sounded serious. "Yes, this is he, "I said.

"Your business is on fire."

WHEN I GOT to the store, the firemen were finishing up.

Their fast response and the sprinkler system had saved the structure and the office. None of the adjacent businesses were damaged. But my showroom and most of the merchandise inside it were destroyed. I asked if I could go inside and remove some valuables, but they wouldn't let me.

All I could think about was that the tobacco card was in there. I pleaded, but they said it wasn't safe. I would have to wait an hour until they would give me the okay.

In the meantime, the fire investigator asked me a lot of questions. "Mr. Quick, we're pretty sure this looks like arson. Is there anyone who might have had a grudge against you?"

Immediately, Simone and Tanya came to mind. "Well there are two roller derby athletes who have threatened me recently."

"Is that how you got those facial injuries?"

"Yes, and one yanked out my tooth." I showed him my mouth.

"Either of them angry enough to do this?"

"You just saw what she did to my mouth. From a woman who would resort to recreational dentistry, anything is possible."

"Were you involved with these two women?"

"Not really. The one who beat me is dating another woman that I was involved with. The other one is just crazy."

"How so?"

"Just interview her, you'll understand."

"Anyone else?" he asked.

"I can think of a few dealers or collectors who might hate me. But not enough to do this. I would focus on the ladies."

"What about you? Where have you been all day?"

"On my couch, asleep. Look at me, I'm in no condition to burn up my own place."

He looked me up and down. He seemed convinced for now. I gave him Simone's contact info and Mandy's so he could chase down Tanya. I was pretty certain one of those two were responsible, I just wasn't sure which one.

When the investigator was done, a TV reporter asked me a couple of questions on camera. I was so stressed by then, I can't remember a thing she asked me. Finally, I got the go ahead from the fire chief and I hurried inside. My heart sank. The metal from the vent cover was warped and there was significant fire damage on the wall all around it. I removed the vent cover and peered inside the hole. There was ash, drywall chunks, and debris on top of the safe. I shoved the clutter aside and pulled out the safe.

At first glance, the case itself was fine, and I was temporarily relieved. But when I spun it around to see the handle and lock, my heart went into my stomach. The handle had melted over and into the lock. Not only that, the sides had melted so the groove where the top and bottom came together appeared to have fused shut. I took it out to my car and got a crowbar to try to pry it open while it was still warm. No luck. My $49.95 safe had protected the card from the fire. It just hadn't protected the card from the safe itself.

4

———

The next morning, I sat in the office of my burned-out store. My head and my mouth hurt, and I wasn't sure how I was going to open the safe. I knew insurance would cover the damage to the store and the value of most of the merchandise. But this was little consolation. Losing the merchandise related to current players was less of an issue. Jerseys and autographs from long dead ball players were irreplaceable. I thought about a collection of lineup cards from the 1800s I had recently acquired. Several museums had expressed interest in adding them to their collections. The cards—and the revenue they would have brought—were gone.

And of course, the card in the melted safe would be disputed by the insurance company if I added it to a claim. Nobody would believe it even existed. Until a few months ago, I wouldn't have believed it.

My computer was destroyed as well. Although all of my contacts and customers were still accessible from my phone, I knew I hadn't been very thorough in backing up my sales information to the cloud.

I sat holding a bat used by soldiers in the Civil War —one of the few things that survived. Memorabilia from this period is rare but gaining in popularity. Last year, an 1860 card depicting the Brooklyn Atlantics fetched enough to buy an average home in Indianapolis and put in a pool. It's hard to believe that before the first drop of blood was spilled in the Civil War, Americans were playing baseball, and making memorabilia.

We're funny creatures, really. We focus on what is lost, and rarely appreciate what we have. The Wagner T206 card wasn't destroyed (even though I couldn't access it). I should have been relieved. Instead, my mind was inventorying what had been destroyed.

I heard the front door open and got up to see who was there. Since I was mourning, it was fitting that I would have a visitor who was dressed all in black. Black shoes, black jeans and a black button-down shirt. On top of that he wore a black leather full length coat.

"We're closed." I looked around the at the showroom, back at him and smiled sarcastically. "We're remodeling."

"I won't take much of your time and I'm not selling anything," he said. "Can we go into your office?"

I sized him up. Mid-fifties, green eyes and short slicked back brown hair. He didn't look like an insurance adjuster and it was too early for the company to have sent someone. More like the manager of a rock band, I thought. Or maybe the owner of strip club.

"Okay, follow me," I said. "And watch your step."

When we got into the office, he shut the door behind him and sat down. "Mister Quick, I would like to hire you to go to Cleveland."

"People call me Quick," I replied. "And did you just ask me to go to hell?"

"No, I asked you to go to Cleveland."

"There's a difference?" I had nothing against Cleveland. In fact, I had never been there. I was just in a vile mood.

"Don't be a smartass. Do you want the job or not?" He paused and looked around the charred remains of my office. "It looks like you could use the money."

"Sorry, I didn't get your name?"

He handed me a card. "Jimmy Chenault," he extended his hand. "I'm with the Brewer Group."

I studied the card and him. The card said the Brewer Group was based in Seattle, but offered nothing about what line of business they were in.

"What is this job in Cleveland?"

"Are you familiar with the Rock 'n' Roll Auction?"

"Yes, but it's not my type of gig. I pretty much stick to baseball memorabilia."

"The artists can donate anything to auction, not just signed guitars and gold records."

I perked up. "And are there any baseball fans in the mix?"

"Sort of. Are you familiar with the Neurotic Meter Maids?" he asked.

"Yes."

"Roxy Bone, the drummer for the band, has a couple of T206s she's donating. Apparently, the band's manager convinced her to buy them as an investment a while back."

"Why is she selling them?"

"She decided to jump on the tiny house/sustainable living bandwagon." He rolled his eyes. "She's getting rid of all the bondages of capitalism."

"Good for her."

"Good for us," he replied. "She has an Eddie Plank and a Cy Young."

"Which Young?"

"Bare hand." This was the second time in less than two weeks somebody had asked me to go to Cleveland and bid on that card. I realized that I never asked the preacher where and when the auction was. Were these the same auctions and the same card?

"Not as valuable as the portrait variation, but still a very desirable card," I replied.

"I would like you to bid on the Cy Young."

"Why not both?"

"I don't need both." I wondered how many tobacco cards this guy actually had. People tend to brag about that sort of thing.

"How much?"

"I'll pay you $3,000 plus expenses to get the card. Your limit is $70,000. I'll pay a $500 bonus for every 10K you manage to stay under that price."

I looked him over and pondered this curious arrangement. Why did he want me to bid for him? "And if I get outbid? A PSA 9 could go into the $90,000 range."

He didn't ask how I knew the card had been graded as a 9. He didn't react at all. This told me it really was the same card the preacher was after. Odd.

He answered, "Three thousand plus expenses. The limit is $70,000, firm. Not bad for a couple of days work —assuming you're driving there."

"Does that mean you won't spring for a flight?"

He snorted and walked towards the door. "The auction is Friday, so you'll need to leave in two days." He looked through the office window and into the show-room. "Is that doable?"

I shook my head. "I don't know. It's going to be hard to leave all of this." At that moment, the wall that separates the office from the showroom fell. Jimmy Chenault was still holding the doorknob, keeping the door and its frame miraculously upright.

He looked back to me in shock. I got up and surveyed the debris. "Yeah, maybe I'll take you up on that gig," I said.

Jimmy blinked a few times and the shock wore off. "Fine, I'll email you the rest of the details." He let go of the knob and the door fell forward. He walked over it and quickly left the building before anything else could collapse.

I suppose I should have laughed, but at the time all I could think about was the priceless card in the little fireproof safe I had purchased for $49.95. I should be kicked in the testicles for buying a safe at Walmart—especially considering the valuable item I had placed inside it. Just thinking about it made me want to crawl into a corner, go into the fetal position, and sob uncontrollably. Because I had to go and purchase a cheap safe, I might never get that card out. I might never sell it. And I might never escape the Simones, the tooth-pulling psychos, and the Jimmy Chenaults of this world. I was depressed.

I found a two-wheel cart and stacked some boxes of recovered items onto it and set the Civil War bat on top. When I was finished, I rolled the cart over the door lying on the floor and through the scorched showroom. I turned back and looked at the store one last time and rolled the cart to my car.

I GOT up early on Thursday to make the five-hour drive to Cleveland. I wanted to get there the day before the auction and get the lay of the land. Since it was a long drive, I called my friend and sometimes life mentor, Rainbow Ruben. Rainbow is half Hawaiian, half Jewish.

He's also not a big fan of being woken up at four in the morning. The time difference between here and Phoenix had slipped my mind.

"Are you in jail, Quick?"

"No, I'm driving to Cleveland."

"So, you're on your way to jail," he replied.

"What do you have against Cleveland?"

"That's where I got food poisoning and had to stay a week in the hospital. I missed five games!" Rainbow played for the Kansas City Royals from 1969-1974.

I shared with him the events of the past few days. "If I can just get that safe open and sell that card, I will be happy. Maybe I can move somewhere warm and watch baseball every day. Maybe do an auction here and there. But mostly, relax."

"Quick, that big payday isn't going to make you happy. I've known you ten years. Settle down."

"Settle down?"

"Yes, you with the women and the drinking and the women." Rainbow repeated words a lot. "You've got to stop. Find a good girl. Marry her. Settle down. Then you'll be happy."

"Rainbow, you've been divorced for fifteen years."

"Some people are happy in marriage. Some people are happy in divorce. You my friend, will never be happy until you get married. Until you live your life for someone other than yourself."

"This isn't the lecture I was expecting to get."

"This isn't the call I expected to get. It's four in the morning, you schmuck."

"Sorry about that, I'll check in with you a little later."

"Be careful, Quick."

All the way to Cleveland, I thought about what he said. I wasn't ready to settle down. But as I took inventory of my injuries and current state of affairs, I had to grudgingly agree that my life needed changes.

THE AUCTION WAS to take place at the Westin near the Rock & Roll Hall of Fame. The hotel's 9,000-square-foot ballroom held the stage, merchandise, and seating area. Items were viewable behind glass counters and display cases. Every fifteen feet or so, there were armed security guards making sure nothing walked out before the auction. I paid ten bucks for a preview catalog, highway robbery if you ask me. But that's how these things go. There were relics spanning the last 60 years of music history. I flipped to an index in the back to find the listing for Roxy Bone. Sure enough, there were two T206 cards there, the Cy Young and the Eddie Plank. On any other day, I might have bid on the Plank myself. But recent events probably were going to make cash a little scarce for a while until the insurance company came through. I couldn't rely on online sales or retail business since my inventory had been wiped out. I would need to work my list of contacts and make money on the fly. Since Kevin didn't have anything to do, I decided to call him as soon as I had verified the Plank was legit.

Unfortunately, that wasn't going to be easy. When I got to the spot where the two tobacco cards were supposed to be, only the Cy Young was there. I studied it and from what I could see through the glass, it looked legit. I called for a member of the staff. After he finished telling a potential buyer all about the Elton John sunglasses collection on display, he directed his attention to me.

"My name is Ryan. How can I help you, sir?"

"I'd like to have a closer look at the baseball cards."

"Of course, sir," he replied and motioned for a guard. The guard moved next to the showcase and Ryan removed the card.

"The catalog pictures two cards. Where is the other?" I showed him that page in the catalog.

"Curious. Let me ask my boss." He texted someone and waited for a response as I examined the Young card. It had been graded and slabbed, meaning that either Roxy or her business manager had sent it to PSA to be graded for quality and authenticity. Sometimes they are right. Sometimes, I'm not so sure. After the card is graded, it's locked inside a plastic slab that protects it from clumsy adults and kids with dirty fingers.

This one seemed genuine, so I handed it back. "Any luck on the other?"

"My boss says it hasn't arrived."

"Weren't they from the same collection?"

"Yes, submitted by Roxy Bone, but only one came in advance. Apparently, her promoter is bringing the other the day of the show. I'm sure if this one is legit, so is the other."

"If they came from the same source, I suppose you're correct."

"You must be a huge baseball fan if you're bidding on those two items."

I lied. "No, I'm just a big fan of Roxy Bone and the Neurotic Meter Maids. That whole punk rock thing does it for me."

"Really, Quick? I bet you couldn't name two of their songs." A familiar female voice taunted me from behind. Ryan looked past me to Valerie Westergren, whose voice I knew without even turning around. For many years, Valerie has been my nemesis. More often than I would care to admit, she's beaten me at an auction. She looks down on me and the other dealers. She's classier, prettier, and better than the rest of us. I hate her. And I'm totally smitten with her.

"Oh yeah? How about '2 Hour Limit,' 'Grease Monkey,' and 'Screech is My Bitch?'" I turned to face her. Her long red hair was pulled back, exposing an elegant pearl necklace and matching earrings. She wore a navy business suit that, combined with the jewelry, seemed overly formal for this gathering. With heels, she stood an inch taller than me.

"Impressive. You know your punk rock better than you know your baseball cards." That hurt.

"What are you doing here, Valerie?"

"Probably the same as you, looking for a tobacco card." She looked in the case, where Ryan had returned the Young card. "Where's Plank?"

"Not here," I answered.

She looked at Ryan, who echoed, "Not here."

She looked at me. "The Cy Young is real," I said.

"I'm not here to bid on it." She looked at Ryan and asked, "Will it be here before tomorrow?"

"I can't say for certain."

"I hope so, otherwise this trip has been a waste." She looked me up and down. "You look like hell. Bar fight?"

"No, I wrestled a bear to save a child's life," I answered.

"You got beat up by somebody's boyfriend, more like it."

"That's not very nice. Why would you say something like that?"

"You smell like bad cologne and bad decisions."

She started to walk away. "See you later."

"Wait, I'm here to bid on the Young, not the Plank."

"So?"

"So, that means we aren't competing. We can be friends. How about a drink?"

She walked back towards me and put her hand on my shoulder. "Let me ask you a question. Do you actually have the song 'Screech is my Bitch' in your iTunes?"

I knew this was a trick question. I had to think fast for the right answer. Not necessarily the truth, but the one that would make her happy. This time, I went with the truth. "Well, yeah."

"That's what I thought." She gave me a mild slap on the cheek. Not the kind you give someone who is rude, the kind you give someone to wake them up. My pain meds had worn off, so it got my attention. "Not a chance."

She turned and walked away. I was speechless and in pain. I turned back to Ryan, who quickly averted his eyes. "I'll see you tomorrow."

"Good luck, Mr. Quick."

"Just Quick."

"Good luck, Mr. Just Quick."

I returned to my room dejected and decided to get room service and turn in early.

5

It was game day. Or auction day, as most people would call it. I was feeling motivated and ready to get out there and win this card. I would have felt better if I were buying for myself and flipping the card to some other collector, but a payday is a payday. Bidding was set to begin at 1 p.m. I arrived a little early to scope out the place. Being that it was the Rock 'n' Roll auction, there were a lot of wannabe rock 'n' rollers milling about. Lots of guys with long hair and black leather jackets accompanied by women with short skirts and black fishnets. If I didn't know better, I would have expected a Bon Jovi concert to be starting soon.

Also included in the potential bidders were the baby boomers. They partied in the '60s, grew up, became respectable, made their fortunes and now wanted to buy back some of their youthful memories. The men of this group wore blazers. The women still wore short skirts and high heels, they just left the leather and fishnets at home. People watching is so entertaining.

Next came the punk rock fans. The true believers, if you will. At an event like this, you run the risk of competing with a true fan who has to own something that belonged to their hero, no matter what the cost. And these true believers can make it expensive for guys like me. However, I was pretty sure that the typical Neurotic Meter Maids fan wouldn't be able to afford a T206 card. But you never know when an obsessed fan with deep pockets might come out of the woodwork.

Most Maids fans would be focused on some of Roxy Bone's drumsticks, tour memorabilia, etc. Of course, the item getting the most attention was a small bone attached to a leather cord. Roxy Bone had worn this human finger bone (phalange for all you medical types) around her neck for nearly five years without taking it off. Now, she was ready to part with it for charity. The bone and strap gave me the creeps. But the steady stream of Maids fans who lined up for a glance practically knelt down to worship it.

As long as that line kept coming, the two cards she had donated were practically invisible to other potentially interested collectors and that was okay by me. I didn't want a whole lot of competition on this. I had enough to worry about with Valerie, because I wasn't buying her act. I was certain she would be bidding on the Cy Young card.

Nearby was a roped-off concession area that still gave me a good view of the people viewing Roxy Bone's contributions. My coffee choices were lousy and lousy with cream. I chose lousy with cream, took another painkiller for my tooth and settled in to people watch. I was half daydreaming and half ogling a couple of female Bon Jovi fans when a face passed in front of me that I recognized. An alarm went off and I didn't know why. The face disappeared as quickly as it had materialized. I couldn't remember who it was or why I sensed danger, but I had to figure out why I felt this way. I quickly navigated the tables of the concession area, held up the rope so I could duck under it and made my way through the crowd. Ahead of me, about twenty-five feet away, I could see the back of the man's head. His hair was black, greased back, and he wore a black leather jacket. He should have blended in with the rest of the rock 'n' roll fans, but he stuck out like a sore thumb to me. I just wasn't quite sure why.

I kept pace and he eventually turned right, following the river of people checking out the items up for bid. It was getting harder for me to keep up. Not that we were going fast, but too many people were crowding in. As he turned, I could see the side of his face. He was late fifties, with the weathered face of a heavy smoker. He seemed nervous, jittery. It was on the tip of my tongue, but I still couldn't spit out the name or why he made me uneasy. Finally, he stopped and looked back over the crowd. Our eyes met. Donnie Duluth!

Donnie's eyes were as big as baseballs when he realized I was looking right at him. He pushed his way out of the stream and towards an exit door. I squirmed and pushed and maneuvered as best I could, but by the time I was free of the crowd, Donnie was long gone.

Donnie's real name is Donald Bradford. But in the business, he's known as Donnie Duluth. Donnie did hard time for forgery in the '90s. He's the best or the worst in the business, depending on your point of view. The best if you're running the scam, the worst if you're the mark. He got the name Donnie Duluth because of the warehouse he had in Duluth, Minnesota, that was raided at the time of his arrest. It was said to have enough fake sports memorabilia to buy The Louvre in Paris and enough fake art to fill it.

I don't know how much of that was actually true, but what I did know made me very uneasy. Donnie Duluth was purported to be an expert at faking tobacco cards. I immediately went back to the Roxy Bone collection and pushed my way through the punk rockers to get to the cards. The problem with punk rockers is, they push back. One particularly surly guy with a nose ring and a purple mohawk wheeled around on me as I nudged my way towards the front. He gave me a shove and the punk rockers started to form a circle. I had to think fast, or I would be visiting my dentist again. I inched my hand up my jacket sleeve and prayed nobody noticed.

I held my other hand up and implored him for

mercy. "My bad, my bad. I just wanted to see my finger one more time before it went up for auction."

Then I lifted the sleeve with the missing hand and prayed that the Maids fans were stoned by noon per usual. There was a gasp from the crowd and purple mohawk tried to make sense of it. "Wait, that's your finger?" He pointed to the glass.

"Yes, yes, it is."

"That means you were the asshole that was two-timing Roxy," yelled one of the female fans. I was still in danger of losing another tooth.

"Yes, that's true. I was that guy. But she forgave me once she saw me like this." I held up the sleeve again. There was some discussion between the female fans as to whether I should be forgiven. However, purple mohawk was satisfied. "Dude, that's pretty rad. My girl caught me foolin' around once. She just broke my stereo."

"Stereo, finger," I answered. "We probably both deserved it."

He laughed and patted me hard on the back. "Hell yes, I deserved it. It was her sister." He chuckled as he walked away, while the crowd parted and let me view my finger. It looked bigger than I expected. Too big for me, if anyone had looked closely. But I didn't think this squad would make the connection. After some fake remorse and contrition, I slid to the right to let the next person admire my encased finger bone. I dialed in on the baseball card. The T206 Plank card was still not there, but I looked the Cy Young card over and over again and couldn't find a flaw. Of course, it was encased in plastic (or slabbed, as people call it in the hobby) and behind glass now, but from there it still seemed legit.

Now I had a decision to make. Buy it and risk it being fake, or walk away. Would my buyer still pay up? Would he demand his money back if it was bogus? Sure, the auctioneer would have to stand behind it, but the legal process could take time and money: two commodities I was growing increasingly short on. I decided to get a drink at the bar and ponder this new development.

WHEN AUCTION TIME CAME, the crowd thinned out. You had to have a ticket to sit in the bidding section, and the gallery around it only held a certain number of people. The rest milled about in the hotel lobby, a combination of fans looking to get a selfie with a celebrity or opportunists hoping to land a wealthy and otherwise unattached businessman. I kept my eyes open for Donnie Duluth and Valerie.

It took an hour to get to the cards. The Cy Young came first. My guess was correct. There were not many people who could afford or were interested in the card. By the time it got to $10,000, I was competing with only two other bidders. Valerie wasn't one of them. I expected her to jump in at some point, but she remained on the sidelines. I was even more surprised when there was no response to my bid of $40,000. The two other guys sat silently. They must have been hoping to get a steal at this non-sports focused auction but didn't have the cash to go high. Valerie still didn't make a play for the card, despite knowing she could get it low and sell it quickly at a profit. When no other bid came, I was happy to know this would be a nice payday, providing the card was real.

The next item up for bid was the Plank card. A door opened at the side of the banquet hall and two men ushered the card in. It was still odd to me that it didn't come with the rest of the items. Since it wasn't available to view the day before, I didn't get to read the provenance of the card. I assumed it came from the same source as the one I had just purchased. The auctioneer was reading off a list of previous owners and I was largely ignoring it while trying to get a better look at Valerie when I heard, "The card was then authenticated by card and memorabilia expert Jonathan Quick who later purchased the card. He then sold it to ..." I didn't hear anything after that.

Authenticators are experts who confirm that the autographs are real, the jerseys are from the proper time period and correct manufacture, etc. When they give the okay, buyers know they are bidding on the real thing.

Was it the pain killers I had taken for my tooth? Was I having hallucinations? Did he really just say *I authen-*

ticated and owned the card prior to the guy who sold it to Roxy Bone? Something was seriously wrong, and all my internal alarms were going off. Then, I caught a glimpse of Donnie Duluth peering out the same door the two guys who had brought the card into the room had exited. Donnie didn't see me, so I got up and slipped out the back of the ballroom. I made my way behind him in the hallway that ran parallel to the room.

When I reached him, I grabbed him by his collar, yanked him away from the door and pinned him against the wall. "What are you up to, Donnie?"

"Nothing, Quick, I swear. Just watching the auction."

"Did you forge that Eddie Plank?"

"I've been out three years, but I'm still on probation. Why would I want to start that up again?"

"Because it's the only thing you know how to do."

"Seriously Quick, let me go."

"Why did the auctioneer say I once owned that card, Donnie?"

"I have no idea."

"Donnie, I'm going to start punching soon."

He looked both ways, scared to death, but maybe not of me. "I'll talk, just not here."

"I need to know now. My friend is about to bid on that card. Not to mention the provenance is a fraud. Do you know how bad this will make me look? My career is on the line here."

He sighed. "You don't know the half of it. Please, let's get out of this hallway before we're seen."

"And my friend?"

"I'm pretty sure neither she nor her buyer will know it's fake."

I let him go and pointed to a small adjacent conference room. The door was open, and the lights were on, but nobody was inside. "In there."

I followed him in and shut the door. "Now what the hell is going on?"

"You got to believe me, Quick, I'm not the brains here. This isn't my deal. They blackmailed me to do the fake."

"Is the Cy Young card real?"

"Yes, it's real. But the Plank and its history are fake."

I studied his face. He was scared and tired. He looked a good ten years older than his actual age. Incarceration and smoking will do that. His salt and pepper hair was receding. So was my patience.

"Why me? Why use me as the authenticator?"

"Because you were bidding on the real card before it."

"I don't follow you."

"You were set up. Now they have your name tied to both the real card and the fake. They wanted it to look like you're in on it so they can blackmail you."

"Blackmail me? What the hell for?"

"They're running a big scam. We're talking millions. I think they're going to auction off real and fake pieces." The more he talked, the more his hands moved. "I don't know who *they* even are exactly. Just the local guys. But this is big, and they have me scared to death. I'm sorry you're in this, but they got me the same way they did you. Made it look like I was part of a scam and forced me in, so I don't get exposed."

"Hell no, I'm not playing for them. I'll let Valerie know it's fake."

"I was afraid you would say that."

6

———————

By the time, I returned to the ballroom, they were auctioning off a guitar destroyed by Sid Mosely of Shackled Fudge. It was in three pieces and appeared to be covered in chunks of brownies and powdered sugar. The auctioneer made allowances that it could be brownie, but it might be covered in feces and cocaine—"you never know with Mosely and the Fudge," he said.

That meant the Plank baseball card sold while I was squeezing info out of Donnie. My heart hoped that someone had outbid Valerie, but my head knew better. Valerie always gets what she wants. When I located her at the table where winning bidders settle their accounts, Valerie stood beaming. "I was surprised to hear that you used to own this, Quick. Why didn't you say anything yesterday?"

More than a few people turned to look at the man

being addressed by this red-headed stunner. That poor slob happened to be me. And I had to think fast. Best not to make any public declarations that could come back on me later. "Not nearly as surprised as I was. When you've been in this business a long time, you can't always remember the items you've examined or sold."

"I suppose that's true," she replied. "But since it's you, I'll always have my doubts."

I glanced around and nobody seemed to be paying attention now. "Who's your client, Valerie?"

"You know I can't tell you that."

"You own it now, what's the difference?"

She laughed out loud. "Does this actually work on other dealers? No wonder you guys are always broke. I don't give out my clients because you hungry little sharks would come gobble them up."

"I'm not interested in doing business with your client." I moved in close. "I just want to make sure you get to keep doing business with him."

She put her hand on my cheek. "Oh, you silly little man. What makes you think my client is a man?" Then she slapped my cheek and walked away.

I don't know if it was the slap or the sight of her walking, but I froze for a few moments. When my mind started to clear, I realized I had two options. Let her take the fake to her client and risk her future. It would be justified, considering she just insulted me, right? Or, I could tell her and have her hate me for not stopping her from purchasing a fake in the first place. Either way, my name was associated with it and that could cost me.

I decided to chase her down. "Please stop, Valerie, we need to talk."

She stopped and turned around. "What do you want, Quick?" She folded her arms and looked me over, "Wait, before you answer that, let me see if I can guess and get all my responses out of the way. No, I won't have dinner with you. No, not tomorrow either. No, I don't want to go to a game with you. No, I don't want to put on a bikini and watch *Bull Durham* with you in a hot tub. Have I covered all your previous requests?"

"*Bull Durham* in a hot tub? I didn't really ask you that, did I?"

She seemed indignant. "Uh, yeah. At the National last year in the hotel lobby. You and a few of your miscreant dealer buddies were doing shots and taking pictures with a cardboard cutout of Nuke LaLoosh."

To be fair, the last night of the National Sports Memorabilia convention (or the National as people call it) is well known for the debauchery. Seemed like an odd thing for me to say when I was impaired. Okay, not odd for me. Just odd for me to say to someone like Valerie. She seemed too strait-laced for that kind of offer.

"I'm sorry," I pleaded. "It was uncalled for. I don't know what I was thinking. *Bull Durham* is certainly not a bikini movie. Lingerie maybe, but not a bikini."

She rolled her eyes. "You're impossible and I don't have time for this."

"I'm kidding. I'm kidding. But I really do need to talk with you. This is serious and it's about that card."

"What about it?"

"Not here, just promise we can meet somewhere quiet later today."

"I'll meet you in public," she said. I didn't like the way she emphasized the word "public." She continued, "Let's say 5:30 in the hotel bar. I can spare a few minutes before I go out to dinner."

"That would be great."

She replied with a dagger, "Dinner with a real gentleman."

"I'm sure he is." I added, "He's probably never even seen *Bull Durham*."

She walked away and tossed a final insult over her shoulder, "Probably why I like him so much."

IN THE MEANTIME, I went to find Donnie Duluth. I wanted to know who these people were and why they wanted me in their little game. Crossing the hotel lobby to exit the front door, I noticed two men looking in my direction. One wore a black suit and tie and looked familiar. The second had a pretentious way about him. He wore a blue pinstriped suit with a bow tie. They both causally turned away when one of the punk rock fans walked by. She had a rainbow mohawk and wore thigh-high leather boots. I should have paid more attention to the black suit guy and less to the woman in leather boots. Maybe Rainbow was right.

My search for Donnie was shorter than expected. He was standing next to a grey van and talking to two guys who looked like they could play football for the Cleveland Browns. He seemed even more nervous than before. When he saw me coming, he nodded to the two tough guys. They both turned and sized me up. I should have run. All the way back to Indianapolis. But as good as I am at detecting antique memorabilia, I'm equally inept at assessing danger. As I walked towards Donnie, they separated and stood on either side of me.

"Hey Donnie, who are your friends?" I looked at them and they said nothing.

"Chatty." I looked back at Donnie. "Let's go grab a drink."

"Quick, I ..."

Tough Guy Number One replied, "Donnie can't have that drink right now. Neither can you."

"Are you sure? I'm pretty thirsty."

"You need to have a chat with Mr. Newton first," he answered.

"Mr. Newton? Doesn't ring a bell."

"Nevertheless, he will see you now."

I was still trying to make them crack a smile. "You ever wonder who came up with the phrase, 'nevertheless'?"

Tough Guy Number One opened the door of the van that Donnie was leaning on. "Get in."

"You know guys, I think they're about to auction off a corset worn by both Lady Gaga *and* Elton John. How about we go and see how much it goes for?" I asked.

Tough Guy Number Two shoved me into the van. "You can read about it tomorrow."

I entered the vehicle face first. Before I could get up, Number Two had a knee in my back, pinning me to the floor. I'm five-foot-eleven, and in fairly good shape. But this guy was built like an NFL lineman. He used a zip tie to secure my arms behind my back. Then, he pulled me up and pushed me into the back of the van and onto a bench seat. I asked, "Will there be a movie on this flight?" He smacked me.

Donnie Duluth got in and took a seat in the middle row. The two tough guys got in the front. Donnie cautioned, "Better keep your mouth shut, Quick." He shrugged his shoulders as if to say there was nothing he could do. I wasn't sure whether to believe him yet or not. At any rate, I was going to meet Mr. Newton.

I EXPECTED to go to some dark warehouse on the bad side of town. Instead, we went to an office park in what seemed to be a nice suburb. There must have been twenty buildings, each with similar uninspiring concrete and glass facades. Most had five to ten office entrances in front, and an alley for deliveries in the back. The van turned into one of these alleys.

Unfortunately, each unit had a number and not the business name on the back side of the building. We pulled up to door number forty and they pulled me out of the van. Next, they led me into a warehouse and through a short hallway past several closed rooms. Finally, they directed me into a finely appointed office and told me to sit.

I waited about ten minutes. My hands were still tied behind my back. I thought about running, but I figured there wasn't much point. I wanted to know why I was here. I wanted to know why they forged the provenance of the Plank card and why they used my name. And, I wanted to know why they had roped Donnie Duluth into this.

Finally, Mr. Newton arrived. He appeared to be about sixty years old, with thick red hair cut in the modern style faux hawk you normally see on guys in their twenties. I thought he looked like the Heat Miser from *The Year Without a Santa Claus*. He wore dark jeans, an untucked gun-metal gray button down shirt, and a distressed-at-the-factory black blazer. He looked exactly like a guy trying too hard to look thirty years younger. On his lapel, I recognized a gold pin. It was the same satellite that Alvin Terrell had been wearing in my store.

He flashed a wicked smile. "Welcome, Mr. Quick. I've been dying to meet you."

"Seems a phone call would have worked much better than this." I stood and moved my arms so he could see the zip tie.

"My apologies." He called out to someone in the hall. "Zeus, get in here." Tough Guy Number One came in. "Cut that restraint off," he ordered. "Our guest isn't a prisoner." He looked at me as if to apologize and said without looking at Zeus, "Mr. Quick is going to make us all a lot of money. And he's going to help us move up in the organization."

Zeus snorted as if to question this prophecy but didn't speak. Newton shot him a disapproving look, yet remained silent. After I was free, Zeus left the room and shut the door.

"Now, Mr. Quick. I have a job for you."

"Go on."

"I want you to forge a list of baseballs, including one signed by Cy Young. Circa 1897. Donnie will handle the provenance documents. When it's done, you pocket $15,000 and expenses. After that, we will no longer need your services and you can head back to Indiana."

"What makes you think I know how to make period realistic baseballs and forge signatures on them?" I asked. "Besides, it's illegal."

"I think you have some experience in this field, or you have a quality source for it."

"I've never faked an artifact."

"Haven't you? There's a guy in New Jersey who says differently." He tossed a picture of a collection of bruises masquerading as a man. His eyes were open and terrified. Blood was running from both corners of his mouth.

"Is that ..."

"Archie Grunwald. Is it coming back to you now?"

"You did that to him?" I stood up.

"Sit down," he ordered. I slowly moved back to my seat. Newton continued, "He did that to himself, by not talking sooner."

Our sins always find us out, don't they? Or is it no good deed goes unpunished? Hell, fill in whatever tired old maxim you want. My past had caught up to me. This may come as a surprise, but I might not have always played by the rules. Confession is good for the soul (see, another well-worn phrase). It happened about seven years ago. Archie was a stand-up guy who got himself into trouble with some gamblers. He put up a Babe Ruth-signed baseball for collateral. The only problem was, he didn't actually have a Babe Ruth-signed ball.

So, I had one made for him. I figured we weren't scamming some honest collector, right? I reasoned this was a degenerate mobster who deserved to have a forged Ruth ball on his desk. Besides, nobody would know, right? And I never spoke of it again. Until now.

"How did you find out?"

"The problem with gambling is that it's a hard sin to give up." I found the religious terminology interesting. "Archie got in debt again and offered up another forged ball as collateral. Only this time it wasn't the same quality as your handiwork."

"And you found out."

"Not me, but someone in our organization. We found out he had put up a ball as collateral before. That one wasn't an obvious fake. In fact, everyone involved insisted it was real. We had our doubts, of course. So, we had to vigorously question Archie."

"So, does the current owner know the Ruth ball is a fake?"

"You mean the bookie Archie fooled the first time? Not a clue. And we didn't say anything because we recognized an opportunity. If someone could create a fake so good it was authenticated, we wanted that guy for ourselves."

"Authenticated? Really?" I felt pride, then guilt. Then pride again. Newton sensed this.

"Pride goeth before a fall, Mr. Quick. Lucky for you, I'm the one hearing your confession, so to speak."

"And if I say no?"

"You and Donnie were seen talking before the auction. A known forger and the guy who validated that card. We have everything we need to pin it on you and nothing to tie us to it. I'm sure that Ms. Westergren wouldn't hesitate to turn you in."

"I can prove I never owned that card."

"Really? I understand all of your purchase and sales records went up in smoke last week." I stiffened up. "I was told you even lost your hard drive in that fire. And that it wasn't backed up."

"How do you know that?" I wondered if they had been talking to Kevin.

He chuckled, "Google, Mr. Quick. The world is at the end of my fingertips. What's at the end of yours?"

I vaguely remembered the reporter at the fire. I don't remember giving her any details about what I had lost. I doubted his source was Google. Most likely, someone back in Indianapolis was prying into my business and sharing it with Newton.

Looking at my hands as I tried to decide what to do, it seemed everything was slipping away from me. I didn't want any part of this, but what choice did I have? "What guarantee do I have that I'm not going to come out of this looking like Archie?"

"Do what you're told. It's that simple."

"I want to sleep on it."

"Take tonight, but I'll expect your answer in the morning."

7

Zeus drove Donnie and me back to the hotel. Neither of us spoke during the ride. However, Donnie slid me a business card and gave me a quick glance as I took it. When we got to the hotel, he opened the door and stepped out so I could exit the van. "Are you coming inside?" I asked.

"I'm not staying at this hotel. Catch up with you later."

Zeus stared at me as Donnie got back inside the van. I winked and blew him a kiss. He simply glared back. Zeus doesn't have a sense of humor, I concluded. They pulled away and I went inside to find Valerie.

I was already five minutes late and hoped she hadn't given up and left. Luckily, she was still in the bar on her phone. She sat alone at a small table, away from the noise and other customers. An untouched martini was the only thing on the table.

"That will be perfect, I'll deliver the merchandise next week." She looked up at me as I sat down across from her. "Oh, you're very welcome. Goodbye now." She hung up the phone and slid it into a Louis Vuitton bag. "You're late," she pointed out as I sat down across from her.

"I was tied up." I held up my wrists so she could see the marks from the zip tie.

"Gross. I would prefer not to know the details of your sordid private life."

"It wasn't that kind of tied up. Some guys kidnapped me."

She didn't believe me. "Really? Who the hell would kidnap you? And why would they return you?"

"The same people who forged that Eddie Plank T206 card you bought today."

She leaned back, crossed her legs, and tried to make sense of what I said.

"I just bought a fake? Please tell me you're making this up."

"I wish I were."

She pulled the phone back out of her bag. "I'm calling the president of the auction company. Or the police." She punched in her code and then stared at the screen, trying to decide her next move. Then she glared at me. "You're guilty too," she said. "Your name is on the chain of ownership for this card."

"It's forged, too," I said. "And that's why I have to ask you not to alert anyone. At least not yet."

"Give me one good reason?"

"I didn't know anything about the card when I got to Cleveland. As you may recall, they didn't include it in the preview yesterday."

"Go on," she said.

"So, I was as shocked as anyone when they claimed I once owned the card. But I had a pretty good idea who was involved when I saw Donnie Duluth watching the bidding."

"Duluth? He's out of jail?"

"Yes. Been out three years already. And he faked the card."

"Three years. Huh, time flies. Well, case solved right?"

"Not so fast," I answered. "He's not the brains of the operation."

"Then who is?"

"I don't know. I met a guy who seems to be pulling the strings, but I'm not sure what the end game is."

"What do you mean?"

"They blackmailed Donnie to do the card and they're blackmailing me to fake some old signed baseballs. They threatened me not to tell you."

She uncrossed her legs and leaned forward with her elbows on the table, close enough for me to smell her perfume. "And yet, here you are."

I smiled, "Here I am."

"And is this supposed to win points with me? Couldn't you have warned me before I bid on the fake card?" She smacked my hand, then looked around to make sure no one had noticed.

"First, I tried to warn you, but the auction was done by the time I was sure it was fake. Secondly, it's not your money. It's your client's."

She was indignant and smacked me again. You would think I would have moved my hands after the first time. "I have integrity, Quick. I'm not taking my client a fake card."

"I'm not suggesting you do. What I had in mind was delaying delivery."

"But this guy isn't buying for the investment. He's trying to complete a set. He's expecting that card in a few days."

"All the more reason to go along with my plan."

"I'm not following you."

"These guys are setting up something big. A large auction with both real and fake pieces in it. The only reason they faked the Plank card was to drag me into this."

"Still not following." I moved my hands off the table in case another smack was coming.

"There must have been a real Plank that they intercepted. Donnie forged the card you just bought, after he got out of jail. Roxy Bone bought her card years ago. These guys must have it."

"So, what's your plan?"

"Well, I don't have all the details figured out yet. But my idea is to switch your fake card with the real one they're probably going to sell along with the other items at this next auction."

"You're crazy," she replied.

"Desperate and currently without a lot of options. But not crazy."

"I don't know," she said.

"Just give me a couple of days to figure this out. Surely you can stall your client. Maybe we can manage to get out of this with both of our reputations intact."

"How did they get you, Quick?"

I looked down at the floor, partly in shame, partly to gather my thoughts. "One time ..." I hesitated. "Just one time, I compromised my ethics to save somebody from a mob-connected loan shark."

"Was it worth it?"

I thought about the question for a moment. "He's still alive," I answered. "But he's still a degenerate gambler."

She leaned back and crossed her legs again. "We could go to the police."

I showed off the marks on my wrists once more. "And what if the police didn't believe us? Or worse, if they told us there wasn't enough evidence? I don't think we're dealing with the kind of people who appreciate involving the police. You don't want to see what they did to my gambler friend."

Valerie took a drink from her martini, set the glass down and stared into it for a while. Finally, she spoke without looking away from her drink. "I've never trusted you in the past, but I'm going to give you a couple of days."

"Thank you," I said. Suddenly, I felt someone standing over me.

Valerie looked up and over my shoulder then smiled. "Stephen? Is it that time already?" She looked at me, "Quick, this is Stephen."

I turned to see a man about six-foot-five with dark brown eyes, dark skin, and dark hair. It was the bow tie guy I saw talking to the man I recognized in the lobby. He looked at me skeptically but offered his hand. "Stephen is an investment banker, Quick."

I extended my hand. "And what do you do, Mr. Quick?" He spoke with either a slight British accent. Or possibly it was the accent of a person with an elite East Coast private education. I wasn't certain which, but knew I wasn't a fan.

"Just Quick," I replied.

"Okay, what do you do, just Quick?" I had never heard so much disdain packed into seven words. Well, at least not from a guy.

I answered, "I harvest organs. It's spleen season in Northern Ohio."

He gave Valerie a puzzled look. She replied, "He's just a memorabilia dealer. We were tending to some auction business, Stephen." She looked at me and glared. "And he was just leaving, right, Quick?"

Just a dealer? I was miffed but didn't show it. I got

up and replied, "Now you two kids be good tonight. Don't stay out too late."

"Run along now, just Quick," Stephen replied while looking directly at Valerie. It was as if he was dismissing one of the help. I walked away with my tail between my legs.

I TRIED CALLING Donnie several times that evening, but he never answered. Finally, he texted me around 11 p.m.

"Donnie, I've been trying to get ahold of you all night."

"I've had the goons watching me all day. And it doesn't help that you're being a wiseass through all of this. They really don't like you."

"The feeling is mutual," I said. "We need to talk. I have a lot of questions."

"I can't talk now, but I will meet you in the morning at Grumpy's Cafe. Think you can find it?"

"Yeah, I'll meet you there at 7:30."

"Be careful," he said. Then he added before he hung up, "And make sure you're not followed."

That was enough to keep me tossing and turning all night. I needed answers. Why was Donnie being watched? Was there a bigger reason behind having me forge baseballs? Why was Valerie dating Stephen? Okay, the last one was easy. It's hard to beat tall, dark, and wealthy.

The next morning, I made my way to Grumpy's Cafe. It's a popular place and usually crowded at this time of the day. Donnie felt this would make it less likely that "they" (whoever "they" were) could put somebody at a table close to us. It took him two cups of coffee and a stack of pancakes to summon the courage to tell me the whole story. By the time he was finished, I wished we had been drinking Irish coffees.

"They're called Satellite," he began.

"Who?"

"This mob, or gang. Whatever they are, I don't know. But the organization is called Satellite."

I asked, "And they're into bogus sports memorabilia? Don't you think they come off a little too 'Italian mob' for a bunch of guys doing fakes and forgeries? I know sports collecting has its underbelly, but it's not usually violent."

"I get the sense they're into a lot of things, Quick. And they are expanding. Recruiting in new cities. That's what this is about."

"What do you mean?"

"This scam they're about to pull off. The one they've roped me and you into. It's an audition by the Cleveland boss so he can move up in Satellite. I listen when they think I'm not paying attention."

"Where is the headquarters? Who is the big boss?"

"I don't know. But it seems like they've got operations all over. A lot of memorabilia from what I've heard, but I picked up a few things about forged art as well. They even said there might be more work for me when this scam is over."

"Really?"

"Yeah, but I don't want to work for these guys, Quick. There's something off about them. I'm not going to pretend I've run with upstanding citizens over the years. I've associated with some bad types in my life. I've even been mixed up with some rough ones, too. But the upper-level guys in this, they're off. I hear 'em quoting Bible verses while planning their scams."

"Kind of like the Samuel L. Jackson character in *Pulp Fiction*?"

"Yeah, but these guys seem to be on some type of criminal higher purpose. Like they've bought into a cult. Give me a cannoli-eating mob boss over these guys any day of the week."

"So, is Newton the guy looking to move up?"

"Yeah, he's the one."

"And what's the scam? Why am I faking baseballs and you're printing cards?"

"The Spider Auction."

"Get out of town. Really?"

"I'm not kidding."

"There is no way they are going to slip a bunch of fakes into the Spider Auction. The Davis Group is running it. They have too many experts on the payroll." The Davis Group is a major player in the auction world and has offices in New York, Chicago, and Los Angeles.

He put down his fork and looked me in the eyes. "Whose payroll?"

"Are you telling me they got to one of the Davis authenticators?"

"I think so. Plus, they plan to make you authenticate the items that are going in. One expert on the outside, one on the inside."

I shook my head. "And if I don't, they let the Italian mob back in New Jersey, the ones you prefer, know they have a fake Babe Ruth ball and the guy who forged it."

"That's the long and short of it."

"How many people do you think know about the Ruth ball?"

"Newton, his boss, probably Zeus. And somebody with Satellite back in Jersey. That group is the one that roughed up Archie."

"And they obviously told you," I said.

"They showed me the picture of Archie. Just in case I needed a little more encouragement to say yes."

"And now we have to create fakes for an auction that will have the eyes of both the baseball world and the art world on it?"

"Welcome to Cleveland."

Long before America fell for the lovable losers known as the Cleveland Indians, there were the Cleveland Spiders. The team played in the American Association from 1887 to 1888 as the oddly spelled Forest Citys or the Blues. Then they moved to the National League and changed their name to the Spiders in 1889. Two years later, they signed Cy Young and steadily improved their win/loss record. By the mid-1890s they were a powerhouse and won the Temple Cup (the precursor to the World Series) in 1895. But in 1899 disaster struck. The owners of the team bought a bankrupt franchise in St. Louis and transferred all of Cleveland's stars to their new ball club. The Cleveland franchise set a record for losses and was ushered out of the league the following year.

The Tarantola family had been minority owners when the Spiders were still competitive and always resented the demise of the team. Apparently, the family had kept a significant number of relics from the period in a private collection that had been handed down through several generations. Now the descendants were ready to sell. The Davis Group landed the prized auction rights and were marketing the collection in an exclusive auction to take place within a couple of weeks. In addition to the baseball items, a significant number of paintings were to be sold.

Donnie explained that Satellite had made a deal with one of the members of the Tarantola family to insert some fakes into the collection.

"Won't somebody in the family know that some of those items don't belong?"

"These are great, great-grandkids who don't give a rip about baseball or this stuff. They just want the cash from the sale. The only family member who knows the true inventory is the one Satellite approached."

"So, the plan is to mix fakes in with the real stuff. And Satellite gets a cut. It still doesn't seem as profitable as selling the fakes themselves."

"It's not about the money," he paused and considered what he just said. "Well, it's partly about the money. But it's also about showing the upper bosses that he can pull something like this off. And do it in a way that doesn't draw attention or leave loose ends. He pulls this off, he and his crew get to move up."

"I've got one more question. Where's the real Plank?"

"What real Plank?"

"The one you used as a model for the fake that sold yesterday. I know you or these Satellite nuts intercepted it."

He grinned. "Nothing gets by you, does it Quick?"

"Where is it?"

"I think they plan to sell it in the auction."

"Again, one more item they could sell directly and get more money from. Why sell it in this guy's family auction?"

"I think Tarantola has some greater value to the organization than just this auction. They're doing everything they can to keep him happy. I just don't know why."

"What does he do for a living? Or is he just living off the trust fund?"

"No, I think he's a lobbyist for a firm that contracts with NASA."

"NASA has an office in Cleveland?"

"Yeah, that's where the Glenn Research Center is located."

NASA and Satellite? This was too much of a weird coincidence. What did space have to do with 100-year-old baseball cards?

8

———

After breakfast, I made my way back to the hotel. Mr. Newton called me just before noon. "Good morning, Mr. Quick. Have you made your decision?"

"Guess I don't have much of a choice, do I?"

"Not really. So, you will need to get started right away."

Just as Donnie had warned, Newton informed me that the job also entailed authenticating some items for the upcoming auction.

"Are these legitimate pieces or more fakes?" I asked.

"It could be a mixture of both. Just mark everything that comes across your table as legit, grade it, and suggest a price."

I asked, "What if it's crap?"

"Then grade it as crap. But legit crap."

I let that thought linger for a moment, then asked,

"What if I just decide this isn't the line of work for me? What if I decide I would rather leave the world of sports memorabilia and become a lifeguard at some YMCA in Arkansas?"

"Mr. Quick there isn't a pool in North America where we won't track you down and drown you. Hell, I'll even throw in your dog, just for spite."

"I don't have a dog. I am thinking of getting a pet mule. Or maybe a cobra with a ..."

"Quick. Shut up and listen very closely. You will do this job. If you don't, we'll frame you for the Plank forgery. Then, when you get out of prison, we'll drown you, your mule, your cobra, and any other pets, friends, and family you might have picked up along the way. Do you understand me?"

I thought for a second. "Yes sir, absolutely. I'll inform the YMCA in Arkansas that neither I nor the mule will be coming. They will be disappointed."

"I'm sure they will get over it. Now get to work on those baseballs."

"I'll need to go back to my workshop in Indianapolis in order to do it right."

"I thought that burned down."

"My store? Yes, it did. But my workshop is in my garage at home."

"Very well. We will have Zeus or one of our other associates check on your progress from time to time. And remember, you need to be back in Cleveland in four days for the meeting with the Tarantolas."

WITH NO OTHER options but to go along with the scam, I called Victor Simmons in Seattle while driving home. The truth is, I didn't make that Babe Ruth ball for Archie all those years ago. I tried. And it was awful. My skills weren't honed, and I needed a fake that wouldn't be detected. I needed Victor. Victor has the devil-given ability to recreate any ball from any era with any signature. So, when I knew I couldn't produce a ball that would get Archie out of trouble, I turned to Victor. Now it was my neck that needed saving and I needed the best.

"Victor, it's Quick."

"Quick, it's been a while. Are you okay? You don't sound like yourself."

"Yeah, I got a tooth knocked out and my jaw is a little swollen. I'm in a bind, Victor. I need some baseballs."

"Are you sure you want to go down that road, Quick? The last time you asked for help you were getting a friend out of a jam. And I warned you that once you crossed that line, you'd be back."

"But you still did it for me, didn't you?" I replied.

"Yes, I did," he answered. "Felt a bit like a Robin Hood moment for me. Sort of a way to redeem myself a bit."

"In some ways it did."

"But now you're back and I feel bad about that.

These balls are to get *you* out of trouble, not somebody else. Am I right?"

I swallowed and answered. "Yes. They are for me. But not for me to sell to someone else. I'm being black-mailed. These guys found out about New Jersey and they want me to produce some more balls for an auction."

"And then what?"

"Then I walk away," I answered.

"You don't believe that, do you?"

"No, not really. But I don't know what else to do right now. Moving forward seems like the only option at this point. I can't go backwards."

"Have you thought about the police?"

"I could do that. But then our little job back east will be exposed. I'm stuck between two mobs, Vic. I've got no way out."

"This isn't an easy thing you're asking me to do, Quick. What if they trace the balls back to me?"

"I've got it covered. I want you to give me all the instructions for doing the balls and let me make a batch here."

"No offense, but I remember that ball you made years ago. This takes skill. Lots of trial and error. Do you really want to bet your life on your own forgery skills?"

"Of course not," I answered. "You didn't let me finish. I'll work on my batch and keep these guys busy. You make the same balls and ship them to me, and I'll switch them out. They won't know the difference. They will see me doing the work but have no idea the finished product is yours."

"Hmm. You sure you can keep me out of it?"

"Yes, you have my word," I answered.

"And payment?"

"Name your price and I'll send it via PayPal."

"$1,000 per ball," he said.

"Done," I replied. They were expensive, but I knew I would sleep better knowing Victor was making them.

"Okay, who do you need?"

"Cy Young, Jesse Burkett, and Bobby Wallace. Oh, and Chief Sockalexis. All on circa 1890s National League baseballs."

"Four balls. How soon do you need them?"

"About ten days. The auction is in two weeks and we need to photograph and display them at the auction site."

"That's tight. Doable, but tight."

"I'm sorry. I know it's a lot to ask, but I'm really in a bind on this one."

"All right, I'll do it," he said. "But remember to keep me out of this."

"I will and I can't thank you enough."

CY YOUNG, Jesse Burkett, and Bobby Wallace each played for the Cleveland Spiders in the mid-1890s. They were also part of the most disgusting trade in history.

The Robinson brothers, who owned the Spiders at the time, bought the St. Louis Browns franchise and promptly traded all the best players from Cleveland to St. Louis. That year, Cleveland lost 134 games and is roundly believed to be the worst team in baseball history. This of course didn't sit well with the Tarantola family, who were minority partners. Within a couple of years, the franchise assets were sold (at a considerable loss) to an ownership group of Charles Somers and John Kilfoyle.

On the strength of their play in Cleveland and later in St. Louis, Young, Burkett, and Wallace would all go on to be inducted into the baseball Hall of Fame. Louis "Chief" Sockalexis would have less of a storybook ending. A Native American, he endured as much (maybe more) racism and bad behavior from opposing fans as Jackie Robinson would half a century later. Sockalexis was a gifted athlete who played for Notre Dame and Holy Cross before his pro baseball career. But inner demons and alcohol would be his downfall. His career ended after only a few brief seasons.

However, Sockalexis' impact was large on the city and young people. At the suggestion of a little girl writing a letter to the owner of the team, the Cleveland franchise in the American League changed its name to the Indians in his honor in 1915.

Baseballs signed by each of these players would fetch a good price if they looked to be authentic. To me, they seemed unnecessary, given the other pieces that were going in the auction. But then again, I had no idea which items were really from the family collection and which were fakes inserted by the Satellite gang.

SIMONE WAS WAITING for me on my porch swing when I got back to Indianapolis. She rocked gently with one foot on the ground, one up on the swing. Her eyes were closed, and she was listening to music on headphones. She wore a tattered Neurotic Meter Maids concert T-shirt, black leggings, and black Converse All Stars.

I nudged her arm, startling her. She vaulted out of the swing into a martial arts pose and I stumbled back. Before I could say a word, she kicked me in the chest, sending me to the ground. For a few moments, I lay on my back and stared at the porch ceiling. I could see her mouth moving, but I couldn't hear. I couldn't breathe. I don't think my heart was actually beating. I was a tilted pinball machine.

"Oh, I'm so sorry. You scared the shit out of me! I didn't know it was you."

"Who else would come home to this place?"

"You're right, but I was jammin' and got caught up in it."

I sat up and looked around. "Why are you waiting here anyway?"

"I wanted to see you."

"The last time I saw you, you threw soup on me."

"Yeah, sorry about that. Sometimes I have a temper."

I coughed and my entire chest hurt. "I think you broke my sternum."

She put her hand on my shoulder. "You poor thing. Are you glad to see me?"

"Sure," I lied. "Really glad you're not holding soup."

She laughed. "I figured with you being out of town, you had time to reconsider."

"Reconsider what?"

"Reconsider us, silly."

I lied again. "You know I've thought a lot about you while I was in Cleveland. However, this really isn't a good time to start a relationship. I just lost my store in a fire. I'm kind of under a tight deadline with a really demanding customer. And, I have to go back to Cleveland. I'm just not in a place where I can be there for you emotionally or physically." I can't believe I came up with that in the moment.

"Well, all of that tells me you need me now more than ever. What kind of girlfriend would I be if I abandoned you when you're down and out?"

I really didn't have the energy to come up with an answer. It took all my creativity to come up with the previous lie. "How long have you been here?"

"Not long, I knew you were almost home."

"How did you know that?"

"The Find My Friends App. I've been tracking you."

"Find My Friends. Doesn't the other person have to give you permission to do that?"

"You did. Well sort of. I set it up at the hospital when you were unconscious from the, you know ..." She pointed to her jaw and then mine. "The tooth."

I shook my head. How much of my privacy had she invaded while I was unconscious? And how much more since then?

She reached out her hand. "Let me help you up."

After pulling me up, she placed her hand on my chest where her Converse had left a footprint. "So sorry about that." She gave me a peck on the cheek and stepped aside so I could unlock the door.

"What were you doing in Cleveland?" she asked.

"I was visiting the Rock & Roll Hall of Fame." I looked at her chest. "Saw some Meter Maids memorabilia."

She smiled back and said, "Come in and tell me all about it."

Simone insisted on making dinner. And since my chest and jaw were hurting, I didn't argue. I was tired from the drive, too, so I unintentionally fell asleep on the couch until I awoke to the smell of pasta sauce and bread. I got off the couch and walked into the kitchen.

"I had all this stuff in *my* kitchen?"

She nodded and smiled.

"Huh, imagine that."

We sat down and actually had a pleasant dinner. Despite the craziness she had displayed thus far, she was well-versed in Indianapolis news, music, and the local art scene. It was a trap. The food, the talk, all of it dismantled my crazy radar. After eating, we cleaned up and moved to the couch. I dozed off and when I awoke, she was asleep and lying next to me. I watched for a moment or two then woke her up.

"I'm going to move to the bedroom and call it a night," I said. "I have a big day tomorrow."

"Okay, I'm ready to go, too."

"I'll see you later," I said.

"No," she said. "I mean I'm ready to go to bed, too."

I wasn't sure what she had in mind, but it was clear she was thinking of spending the night. I was feeling too much pain and exhaustion for any sort of playtime. "Look, I don't think that's a good idea. I'm going to be asleep in minutes."

She laughed. "It's okay. I know you're too banged up for me to rock your world." She said that like I wouldn't be able to handle her in the bedroom. And I'll admit, for a moment I was intrigued. But I was also feeling the pain meds for my tooth wearing off. "I just don't feel like driving home now," Simone said.

In my weakness, I said, "Okay, you can stay tonight."

"What do you want to do tomorrow?" she asked.

"The first thing we need to do is go to the hardware store."

You might be wondering how to make a baseball look like it's 100 years old? First you start with an old baseball with no markings. Vic has mastered the technique of stamping and even changing the thread colors of baseballs, but for today's lesson, I'll keep it simple. Just pick up a used baseball at your local Goodwill or Salvation Army thrift store. Look for one with no markings. Wash the ball with soap and water. Once it is dry, you sign the ball, using an example of the player's signature as a guide. Vic, of course, uses pens and even ink that are period specific.

Next, "dip" the ball. Back in the day, people used to shellac baseballs they thought were valuable. They didn't have UV protected ball cubes 100 years ago. So, if you had a baseball signed by Rogers Hornsby, for example, you would dip it into shellac in order to preserve the autograph and your prized possession. And dipping is what forgers do today. Just stick a nail in between the seams of the ball (not too deep), hold it by the nail, then dip it in a rust colored shellac and hang it to dry. Once it's dry you have to get the smell of new shellac out of it. So, you bury it in a bag of dog food for a few days, then put it in sunlight to cure. Or you can leave the ball in a bag of mothballs. After a few days, it looks old. It smells old. And now you have a decent forgery. Of course, there are some steps I've left out, just so you don't get the urge to do this yourself. I wouldn't want your future life of crime to be on my conscience. Unless, of course, you're cornered by the mob. Then look me up.

ON MY THIRD day back in Indiana, Mr. Newton called to tell me someone would be checking on my progress. I expected to see Alvin Terrell drop in, since he was wearing the same pin when he came to my store. Instead, a thug who looked and dressed much like Zeus knocked on my door.

"You Quick?" he grunted.

"Yes, come in," I said. "You must be with Satellite. Are you from the Indiana chapter or the home office?"

"Show me your balls."

"If you want to see those, you're going to have to buy me dinner," I replied. "Take me dancing even. What kind of guy do you think I am?"

He pulled back his jacket to expose a gun in a holster. "The balls. I'm in a hurry."

"Oh, you want to see the *balls*. Right this way." I motioned for him to follow me and made my way to the garage. "Watch your step," I warned as I opened the door and turned on the light.

He looked at the floor. There was no step. No threshold or transition between the hallway and the garage where one could trip. "Why?"

"Just something I like to say to avoid litigation."

He didn't smile.

"See for yourself." I pointed to four balls that were lined up and drying on a portable table in the middle of the garage. It smelled of lacquer and dog food. The forged signatures were on the baseballs, but they still looked new.

"These look awful."

"They are aging. I showed him sandpaper, a hair dryer, and multiple open cans of stains, varnishes, and oils. "It's a complex mix of items, and I have to do a series of coats over the next few days and then dry them completely in between."

He looked at me skeptically. "Trust me, these will be done in time for the auction and look good enough to fool anybody," I said.

"Bring one to Cleveland Thursday. The boss wants to see how far along you are. It's him you have to convince, not me."

"Okay, I'll do that. But it won't be ready."

"Doesn't matter to me," he said. "I'm not the boss."

He walked out of the garage and back down the hall towards the front door. He was detached. None of this mattered to him. He was just there to do the inspection and report back.

"Sure, you don't want a drink for the road?"

"Just bring the ball."

"It was an honor to have you look at my balls."

He glanced back and glared. "Just bring the balls."

Must be a real hoot to work for these guys, I thought. What's the point of being in a cult if you can't have any fun?

9

———————

As promised, I returned to Cleveland on the fourth day and brought two baseballs with me. The first was one of the balls I was working on in the shop. The second was a fake someone had left at the store—a Ted Williams ball from 1938. Overall, it was a pretty good forgery, but I had spotted a few problems. A guy had come into the store and claimed he purchased it on eBay for $500. He had lost his job and now he needed some quick cash. When I told him he had been duped, he stormed out of the store, leaving the baseball on the counter. I thought I would show it to Mr. Newton and pretend it was one I did. The Williams ball, I would claim, would be what the finished product would look like. He wouldn't know the difference and it would buy me time.

After checking into the hotel, I called Zeus and changed into a suit. Both of which I had been instructed to do by Newton. Thirty minutes later, the Satellite henchman picked me up outside the lobby. He didn't get out and open the door for me. I was pretty certain if I had been the boss, Zeus would have opened the door.

I slid into the seat and placed a bag with the baseballs on the floorboard. He must not have noticed. Then, I ran my right hand over the left side of my suit jacket, like a model showing off the tailoring. "I got all dressed up and you didn't even open the door for me. What kind of date are you?"

"Did you bring the ball?" he asked.

I held up the bag. "Two of them, in fact. Don't you know they come in pairs?"

He scowled at me. No sense of humor.

We arrived at the Tarantola estate just as the sun was going down. Lights set to timers began to come on around the grounds, preventing the darkness from hiding the sprawling house. It looked more like a hotel than a home. Constructed of whitewashed brick with a red roof, it reminded me of George Washington's Mount Vernon estate. There was a large circular drive in front of the home. Two smaller structures of similar design flanked the main building.

A valet took the keys to the car, and we followed a couple in a tux and gown into the main entrance. In a family as wealthy as this, I learned, multiple gatherings may very well be happening at the same time. Tonight, the matriarch of the family was throwing a fancy dinner party. I later found out it was a private fundraiser for the Great Lakes Wildlife Foundation. We were quickly steered away from it and into a side chamber. There I found Donnie, Mr. Newton, and a man I assumed to be a Tarantola. Spread across multiple tables were items from the family collection.

Newton introduced us. "Nick Tarantola, meet Mr. Quick."

Nick Tarantola was not the stereotype of an Italian mob boss that I expected to meet. Instead, he had the air of a distinguished actor. Think George Hamilton, without the deep tan. His hair was grey with some unusual jet-black streaks on the sides that had apparently resisted whatever eminent domain battle the rest of his hair had lost. Physically he was fit for his mid-sixties and looked like he could give Zeus a battle if it ever came to it.

But he didn't look like a mobster. Or whatever preconceived image I had of a mobster. I suppose I shouldn't have been surprised by that, because with the exception of Zeus and the other henchman, nobody in Satellite had looked mobsterish. By no means do I mean to imply Tarantola looked innocent. However, he seemed more devious than diabolical. Devious I could navigate, diabolical, not so much.

"Welcome to my home, Mr. Quick."

"I would say thank you, but I don't particularly feel any gratitude."

Zeus stepped forward to address my ingratitude. A

glance from Tarantola held him off. "And why is that?" he continued.

"I'm being forced to work for you. To commit a felony. Excuse me if the work I'm doing for you doesn't inspire feelings of loyalty and respect."

He chuckled. "You may come to find that working for us agrees with you. But in the meantime, I understand your predicament. Let's have a brief look at the items and then have dinner. After a meal, I might not seem so sinister to you."

There were to be five groupings of items in the auction. The proceeds of two groupings would go to the family as a whole —items agreed upon by all of the descendants. Another group of items came from the private collection of Nick and his wife. Group four belonged to a daughter of Nick's brother. The final group contained paintings by the Dutch Impressionist Vinke. Some of the proceeds from this group were going to charity, some to a trust, and I honestly can't tell you the rest. As soon as he started talking paintings, I tuned it all out.

My attention was focused on the baseball treasures at hand. There were scorecards, gloves, baseballs (signed and unsigned), pictures and other artifacts. Nick was particularly proud of a dozen daguerreotypes of supposed Cleveland players.

"All of these men played for my great grandfather's baseball team. These should fetch a good price at the auction. And they are legitimate pieces," he glanced at me, then at Newton. "Not the dross you two will be creating."

"They are valuable. But they didn't likely play for the Spiders."

He sized me up. "Are you sure, or just trying to bust my balls?"

"No, I'm sure. Daguerreotypes were on the way out by the mid-1860s and your family didn't own the team until the late 1880s."

"So, they're worthless?"

"On the contrary. These are Civil War era ballplayers. And that period is on the rise with collectors. These will sell quickly at auction."

He appreciated my candor, and this told me that even though Nick was driving this process for the family, he was not an expert on any of it, save the art. This would be to my advantage later, I hoped.

As I chatted with him and got to know more about the family, he shared that the Tarantolas never forgave the Robinson brothers for destroying the team. Over the years, the two families had a feud rivaling the Hatfields and McCoys. But instead of it playing out in the hills of Appalachia, it was waged in the boardrooms of Northeast Ohio, on golf courses and yacht races, and in the society gossip columns of newspapers. This hate had not dissipated over the course of 100 years. Not in the least.

Mr. Newton pulled me aside. "I think he likes you, Quick."

"Oh yeah?"

"Yes, and that's good for all of us. After dinner you will come to the back room and go to work authenticating and pricing the baseball-related items. What you don't finish tonight, you can do in the morning as Zeus will collect you at your hotel at 8 a.m. sharp."

"Will he bring coffee? Maybe a muffin?"

"Tarantola likes you. I don't. Remember that. Also, we need you to work quickly. They're still getting pictures for the website and auction catalog and need to get it to the printer."

"And when I'm finished?"

"Once you're done, you are free to return to Indianapolis for the weekend, but we will expect you back by Tuesday with the baseballs. You'll help with the preparations and setup for the auction and stick around to answer questions from the attendees as our resident third-party expert. Then you may leave."

"With a check for $15,000, of course."

"But of course. Provided the balls all sell without the slightest concern for their authenticity from the buyers."

"Naturally," I said. "Actually, I'm not very hungry. How about I get started on the items?"

"Oh no. I insist you join us. Nick is amused by you. And he has lots of questions about fake autographed baseballs."

"Before we do, I have one more question."

"Okay."

"What the hell are we really doing here?"

"What do you mean?"

"I mean this isn't how auctions work. I've been around long enough to know this." He stared blankly back at me. "Usually this stuff is appraised, professionally photographed, and cataloged in print and online. Then they market it for at least a few months to drum up interest. This is all so haphazard and last minute, I can't believe the Davis Group is involved."

Newton laughed, "Yeah, we have pretty much violated every term of that contract, but they haven't pulled out because they want the payday."

"Why not play it straight? I thought you had a guy on the inside."

He looked at me funny and I knew I shouldn't have said that. He knew Donnie told me. "That was how it was supposed to work. But we had to move up the timeline on the launch."

"The launch?"

"Never mind. The point is the Davis Group agreed to manage the auction the day of and stay out of the rest. We've given them enough to promote the auction but not enough to see the total number of items and what they are. It's driving them nuts and they almost walked away from it, but they know they can't. Some guy in the marketing department broke the news before the ink had hit paper and now, they don't want egg on their faces. But all that works to our advantage because they can't tell what fakes we're putting in."

"But they have authenticators. Surely, they are going to figure it out."

"That's why you're here, genius. The Davis Group is standing down because of your reputation. If you say it goes in, then it goes in. And you will say it goes in. All of it."

I was speechless. They had every angle covered. At least, as far as I could tell in the moment.

"Now," he continued, "let's eat."

I was led into a room with a large dining table. Servants bustled about and an additional half dozen people looked to be joining us. Apparently, none of them were invited to the fancier dinner going on somewhere else in the house. The smell of whatever was about to be served told me that I was hungrier than I had let on. As everyone was being seated, I decided to excuse myself to the bathroom. I didn't want Nick asking me too many questions and hoped he would sit next to someone else while I was gone. A staff member walked me to the bathroom, which was a couple of hallway turns away. When I was done, I made my way back to the dining room. Ahead of me in the hallway, I heard the click clack of high heels.

I first saw her from behind. A deep blue dress hugged her curves and bright red heels popped in a room full of conservative shoes and conservative colors. Her dress was strapless and when she pulled her hair to one side, she revealed a spider tattoo on her right shoulder. But what was most striking was what she carried in her right hand—a baseball bat. I didn't speak. Hell, I couldn't. She was breathtaking and I hadn't even seen her face or anything else from the front for that matter. She was beautiful trouble. I should have been more concerned about the bat.

Emily Tarantola strode confidently up to the empty chair next to where Nick was sitting and tossed it out of the way. Then she swung the bat, shattering a crystal decanter with a baseball stopper located in the center of the table. She dipped her shoulder a bit, but the swing was pretty good. Perhaps if I took her to a batting cage .... At any rate, she had everyone's attention.

Pointing the bat in Nick's face, she said, "That damn brooch is mine. It's not going into the auction." She then took the time to glare at each person in the room, one at a time. As she did, she pointed the bat. "Is that clear?" I don't know about the rest of them, but it was clear to me. Nick didn't speak, and Emily marched out of the room.

When she got to the door (where I was still standing transfixed), I said, "You dropped your shoulder on that swing."

"Your pants are unzipped," she replied without stopping or looking me in the eyes.

I COMPOSED MYSELF, zipped up and headed to dinner like nothing happened. When I sat down, Nick apologized. "My brother's child. Her mother is Irish. It's a volatile combination, the Italians and the Irish." He gestured towards the shards of glass. "Things get broken."

I was looking towards the hallway where she had disappeared. He leaned in and whispered, "She's dangerous, my friend. Do your job and go home. Or *you* will get broken." He turned his head to the mess on the table and said no more until the collateral damage was cleaned and the food arrived.

For an Italian family, the chef made excellent Chinese stir-fry. After the meal came, Nick shared more family history. "Did you know my family took the name Rogers when we got to America?"

"I did not. How come?"

"Italian-Americans were hated by many in those days. There are exhibits in the Baseball Hall of Fame that put a spotlight on the bigotry that kept blacks out of the game," he said. "But you will find no such discussion of how Italians were persecuted near the turn of the century."

"I suppose you're right. It's not a subject that comes up much."

"Did you know that eleven Italians were lynched in New Orleans in 1891?"

I gulped. I was afraid he was about to say someone named Quick was responsible. "No, I never knew that."

"It was the worst lynching in American history. And

it's mostly forgotten. But I haven't forgotten how America treated my people."

"Tell me about what you do for a living," trying to change the subject.

"I'm a negotiator."

"Someone told me you were a lobbyist." That someone was Donnie, and Google confirmed it.

"Isn't that the same thing?"

"And you focus on space policy?"

"I connect private enterprise concerns with the technology and expertise of NASA engineers."

"Is that lucrative?"

"Look around you, Mr. Quick. I may have inherited this place, but it takes a lot of money to keep it."

I looked around the room again. "Fair enough."

I managed to get through dinner without him asking me any difficult questions, then excused myself to go back to work. I intentionally got lost, just hoping to run into Emily. It didn't take long. I found her in a small reading room. She was still wearing that mesmerizing dress and sitting on an antique sofa. Next to her was a cocktail glass with a couple of ice cubes in it.

"I've zipped up."

"Thank God for that." She glanced up from her magazine. "Can I help you?"

"I'm here to appraise the artifacts for the auction."

She turned back to her magazine. "Then go appraise."

"But I have a question."

She put the magazine on her lap and leaned back. "What?"

"From that little bit of batting practice you did back there, I gather there's something you don't want to have sold. I just want to make sure I separate it out from the other items."

That got me a wicked little smile. "It's a spider brooch. It's mine, Grandmother gave it to me. I don't care what these other people tell you."

"Right, right. I didn't see it when I looked the room over the first time, but if it's a brooch, it could have been easily overlooked. Do you have a picture?"

"No, but it should be the only spider-shaped jewelry piece in the collection." She sat forward and lowered her voice. "If you find it, slip it in your pocket and bring it to me." She arched a brow and smiled. "I'll make it worth your while."

I'm pretty sure she had no idea how much my while was worth at that moment. "I believe you could at that."

From behind me a voice called, "That dress is hideous."

I was so enthralled by this woman that I didn't hear the gentleman standing to my left approach. I turned and he was wearing a black dinner jacket with a purple sequined bow tie. He looked me up and down.

"So is that tie," she replied without introducing me.

"Bitch," he responded.

"Don't you have a cocktail getting warm somewhere?"

He glared at her, then looked me up and down once more. "Who dresses the help? I mean seriously?"

With that he was gone, and Emily went back to reading her magazine like neither of us had been there. I was bewildered by this family. But I wasn't giving up.

"Tell me about the history of this brooch."

She looked up again from her magazine. "It originally belonged to my great-great-grandmother. My grandmother assured me it would come to me, but you know how families can be." She paused as if waiting for my affirmation. I had no idea how this family could be. She continued. "It's blue and gold with rubies and sapphires on the legs. On the spider's back is a large sapphire surrounded by diamonds."

"I'll be on the lookout."

"If you do find it, make sure it gets to me." She kept talking but looked back at her magazine. "If it disappears from this house, I'll assume you stole it."

"I assure you, I won't steal it."

"I'm glad to hear that." She looked back up from her magazine, "Because if you do, I'll take some more batting practice." She looked me up and down. "And I'll be sure not to drop my shoulder."

Before I could respond, we were interrupted by a butler bringing her a fresh drink. "Jeffrey," she said without looking at him, "this man was just leaving. Could you help him find his way out?"

"Very well, miss."

"Mister?"

"Quick."

"Mr. Quick then. Will you follow me?"

"To the ends of the earth." He looked puzzled. "And to you Miss Emily," I said, "I'll consider your offer."

"It's not an offer. It's an order."

Jeffrey nodded to me as if to say, "all of her offers are really orders."

"I'll consider your order."

Jeffrey seemed in a chatty mood as we left Emily to her drink and magazine, so I got him to show me various antiques and divulge some family history. No sordid tales, of course. Just the things he deemed an uncultured Hoosier would need to know. I let him drone on since I really didn't want to meet up with Zeus again to start appraising. Besides, delaying might catch me another glimpse of the fair Emily.

One particular showcase drew me in. He told me the history of several of the silver pieces. Some were wedding gifts, some were awards and miscellaneous trophies. I'm sure if I cared I would have been impressed. But one piece seemed to be poking out of the back, trying to stretch its neck to be seen if you will. It began to give me heart palpitations. I pretended to be curious about the piece in front of it.

"What is that large silver platter on the bottom shelf, far left?"

"It was given to the family by Umberto the First, King of Italy, not long before his death in 1900."

"Wasn't he killed by an anarchist?"

"You know your Italian history."

"I know my anarchists." He gave me a strange look. "So, how about a closer look?"

"You are a stranger, sir. I only take these out for family."

I looked both ways. "Look, I'm never going to be here again. So, I'm never going to be this close to something owned by an actual European monarch. Hell, for all I know Umberto used this to serve pizza while he was watching Christians being devoured by lions."

"I take that back," he replied, "you really don't know your history."

I really did, but I thought the intentional gaffe might make him keep talking and give me an opportunity to get a closer look at the piece in the back.

I shrugged. "How about a look? I'll keep my hands behind my back, and you can even put my phone in your pocket, so I won't take pictures."

He thought for a moment. "Very well then." He produced a key from his pocket and unlocked the case. Then he pulled out the silver platter and held it up. He droned on for about five minutes and I pretended to care. My main goal was to get a good look at the trophy, long forgotten, behind it. As he reopened the case, I stepped closer to the glass and studied it, preventing him from opening the door wide enough.

"Sir, if you don't mind."

"Oh, pardon me. I just noticed there was an item behind it."

"Yes, the wife of the late Robert Tarantola hated that piece and instructed the staff it could stay but must not be visible. Eventually her husband forgot about it, I suppose. No one ever asks about it and we don't discuss it when entertaining visitors. I doubt anyone even remembers why it's there."

I didn't ask him to show it to me. That would be too risky. If he knew it was related to the Cleveland Spiders and the items in the auction, he might blab to someone. But I knew what was only inches from my grasp. It was the Temple Cup: the original world championship trophy of baseball. The prize awarded to the winner of the precursor to the modern World Series.

10

Remember the night before Christmas? How you couldn't sleep because that Red Ryder BB gun or the Malibu Barbie was so nearly in your hands? Just a few more hours and it would be yours. You couldn't wait to push aside the gifts wrapped for your siblings and get to your long-awaited treasure. You were dying to rip off the shiny paper, tear open the box and touch the amazing toy inside that would change your life forever.

That's how I was feeling the rest of the night and into the next morning—all because of a forgotten trophy hidden behind the family's silver heirlooms.

So, why did this piece of history have me sleep-deprived, unfocused, and ready to do anything to get it? Because this was like finding out there's a second Lost Ark of the Covenant! Not only does it exist, it's in a glass case in a suburb of Cleveland! Which made it currently more accessible than the priceless baseball card locked inside my melted Walmart safe.

Men are by nature competitive. They vie for trophies, build monuments to their successes, and even put notches in their bed posts for ... well, you get the idea. Male achievements are not trees falling in the woods without a sound. If a guy did it, somebody is going to hear about it.

In 1894, the guys who ran the National League (the most successful professional baseball league at the time) decided that a winner at the end of the season wasn't enough to placate their egos. There needed to be some type of extended competition. They required something more grandiose to put an exclamation point on the long baseball season. Like most male achievements, it must be perceived by others as much grander than it really is. They decided to call this extended competition the World Championship Series. They chose this name even though their league consisted of twelve teams located from the East Coast of the United States to St. Louis. There were no teams in the South or West and none outside the United States.

Having an ostentatious trophy to commemorate this new championship was a must. As I said, this was a guy thing, and all guy things must include a large trophy. This particular trophy was donated by a co-owner of the Pittsburgh Pirates, William Chase Temple. And in guy fashion, he insisted this custom trophy he had commissioned for $800 should have his name on it.

Thus the Temple Cup was born. This new post-season best-of-seven series would be played by the top two teams in the National League from 1894-1897. I have no idea why they decided upfront that it would only go until 1897. The team that won the series got to keep the Cup for the year. If any single club won it three of those four seasons, it would have permanent ownership of the Temple Cup.

If this sounds somewhat familiar, it should. This was the invention of the playoffs. Cleveland won the Cup once, in 1895. After the 1897 Temple Cup Series, the trophy was returned to William Temple, as no team had won it three times. It remained in the Temple family for many years and was even loaned to the 1939 World's Fair for display. Several years later, his descendants sold it to the Baseball Hall of Fame for just $750. That's $50 less than it cost to make and considerably less than the $21,300 it would have cost to produce in today's dollars. Of course, that doesn't come close to what a collector would pay if he got his hands on the Temple Cup, now sitting in the home of the Tarantola family.

One of my first challenges would be to determine if this was the original or a copy. A copy wouldn't fetch much, unless I could somehow prove it wasn't modern but made by the same company during the same time period. It would not be outside the realm of possibility for one of the owners of a team that won the Cup to commission his own copy during the season he had it in his possession. Men don't like to give up their trophies—even for a bigger trophy. Given the choice, they would find a way to keep both.

This would be tricky research. I wouldn't want to alert too many people that a second trophy might exist. There would be a feeding frenzy in the collectibles world. The biggest hurdle to authenticating the trophy was this: the only person who could confirm which was the original and which was the copy had long since died. Another thing to consider was which was the original? Was it the one in the Tarantola showcase or the one in the Hall of Fame? And since Cleveland had multiple owners, were there multiple copies? Going to Pittsburgh to research it was out of the question while the Satellite crew had me by the autographed balls. Despite these obstacles, I was determined to get my hands on that trophy.

These were the thoughts running through my head as I worked through the merchandise destined for the auction. I was also making a mental note as to which items I could secure for my own clients. I wouldn't be able to bid, but that didn't mean I couldn't split the commission with someone who could. I wouldn't be able to use Kevin. If they knew this much about me, they probably would spot my one and only employee. However, I had a friend and fellow dealer in Cincinnati who wouldn't mind making a few extra bucks for helping me out.

I made it through about 60 percent of the merchandise by 11 p.m., then signaled Zeus that I needed sleep. So far, I hadn't found the spider brooch.

The next morning, I was back at it early. The mansion was quiet compared to the night before. Zeus and Jeffrey ushered me into the room with the auction merchandise. I was disappointed when I didn't see Emily anywhere along the way. Zeus was all business. He handed me the bag of baseballs I brought the night before and told me to get busy. Whomever Mr. Newton had shown them to for approval, they must have passed the test. Then he went to a bench on the opposite side of the wood-paneled room and sat down to read the paper.

I had appraised most of the larger pieces during my first visit. Today, there were many little items to plow through. Much of it was of value only to the most hard-core Cleveland fan. Some would appeal to any baseball historian, and some I could see on display in the Baseball Hall of Fame in Cooperstown. Although most were from the period when the Tarantola family was directly involved in team ownership, many came from the eras before and after. It seems the family's love of the game was more than a passing fad.

One item stood out on this visit. Someone had wrapped a painting in brown paper and the word *portrait* was written on the outside in black marker. The ink was faded, and the wrapping smelled like a cellar. The entire package was dusty, and I left fingerprints as I turned it over to decide where to open it.

I found a taped seam and gently pulled. The old tape was so brittle, it opened with ease. I slid the painting out of the wrapper to reveal a 10-by-14 portrait of Chief Sockalexis. It was painted by a man named Herman Trent and signed on the back. Taped to the frame of the canvas was a small box. This tape and the box looked modern. The painting could have been commissioned when the chief was still alive. I looked to make sure that Zeus was focused on his newspaper. Then I gently ripped the tape and pulled the box from the frame. I opened it and glanced back at Zeus. He had no interest in what I was doing, so I pulled open the tissue paper in the box. It revealed a jewel-encrusted spider brooch. The very one Emily said she would make worth my while, if I handed it over to her.

The spider was made of gold (24-karat, I assumed) with a deep blue guilloché enamel back. Gold outlined the body and each leg had a small ruby at the joint and sapphires at the tip. A dark blue sapphire was surrounded by multiple diamonds forming a "C" in a custom setting on the back. The head had two more rubies for eyes with additional diamonds surrounding them.

I wasn't an expert in jewels or antique jewelry but seeing the brooch in person made me realize why Emily was willing to destroy the serving crystal to get her hands on it.

Another glance at Zeus and I was confident he was still oblivious to me. I put the lid back on the box and slipped it into the pocket of my blazer. After a couple of hours, I told Zeus I was finished. He took the list from me, told me to wait there, and went to find his boss.

I didn't wait there. I can honestly say I wasn't sure which I wanted to see most: The Temple Cup or the lovely Emily. Both were beautiful in their own way. Both were worth a fortune. Both were going to get me in a lot of trouble.

The night before, I had decided to help Emily. I also had decided to acquire the Temple Cup—by honest means or otherwise. If I couldn't strike a deal with Emily, maybe the butler could be convinced to assist. At the very least, maybe he could be distracted.

I found Emily first. Or I should say she found me first. I was wandering the halls of the giant home and suddenly a hand grabbed me by the shirt and pulled me into a sitting room. Initially I thought it was Zeus and I dropped the bag of baseballs with a thud on the wood floor. But when the light came on, I was surprised to see the beautiful heiress.

"Did you find the brooch?" she asked.

I answered with the question that had puzzled me the night before. "Can I ask why you didn't just go into the room with the auction items and take it? You don't strike me as the type of person who would be afraid to do that."

"My uncle is keeping it locked up. Only he and one member of the staff has a key. Besides that, I know it's hidden, so it might not be in there. If it is, it might be hidden somewhere so that even you don't see it. He's selling it for spite as much as for the money. We don't get along."

"You couldn't convince the servant to help you?"

She twisted a curl of her silky black hair and sighed. "He wouldn't succumb to my most earnest attempts to sway him, if that's what you mean."

That wasn't what I meant. But now I could see she had no problems using money or other enticements to get what she wanted. I remember thinking that might come in handy. Some days, I'm a bona fide idiot.

"Suppose I was able to locate it. You mentioned you could make it worth my while."

She licked her lips, took a seat on the couch, patted the seat next to her, leaned back and crossed her legs. "My dear Mr. Quick, whatever do you mean?"

This was going to take all the restraint I had inside me. I had made up my mind that I wasn't going to settle for a fleshly reward. However, I figured just a little taste wouldn't hurt. I joined her on the small loveseat. Before I had even leaned back, she had ahold of my shirt and her tongue in my mouth. She paused long enough to say, "Let's make this quick, I've got a massage scheduled for 1:30." She paused and chuckled at herself. "Quick, get it?"

If I had a dollar for every time ...

I tried to interject as she commenced unbuttoning my shirt while my blazer was still on. "I haven't shown it to you yet."

She unzipped my pants, "Patience, I'm getting there."

"I meant the brooch!"

"Oh, yeah. I do get a little impetuous."

"I noticed that last night," I said. "I was able to find it."

She glanced at the bag of baseballs, then back at me. "I believe you, now take your pants off."

"But I had something else in mind."

She looked down at her chest, with blouse now open and bra showing. "Seriously, you're going to turn down this for money?" She pulled her hair to one side, "Trust me, Quick. I know men and you'll just piss the money away." She leaned in close again and nibbled on my ear. "You won't forget the next 30 minutes for the rest of your life."

I pondered this bold declaration for the next minute or so as she continued as if it was a done deal. From somewhere deep inside, I summoned the willpower. "Actually, I was thinking of a different kind of trade."

She leaned back and gave me a puzzled look. After staring at me for a few seconds, she said, "Oh, no. Last night I was sure you were trying to hit on *me*. I can't believe you of all people would be into my cousin Frankie?" She stood up, disgusted. "How did I misjudge this?"

"Frankie, who's Frankie?"

"My gay cousin," she replied. She could see I wasn't following. "The guy who said my dress was hideous."

"Oh, sequin bow tie?"

"Yes, is he the kind of trade you had in mind?"

"No." I thought for a second. "No! I'm sure Frankie's a swell guy, but that's not what I have in mind. I want to trade the brooch for something else."

Now she was really offended. I'm guessing that outside of the butler, she wasn't used to being turned down. "Then what do you want?"

"There's another piece in the collection that I want. I'll trade you the spider for this relic."

"Why would I trade you a family heirloom for another family heirloom?"

"Besides the brooch, are there any other items in the collection you care about?"

"Not a single thing."

"Then what does it matter?"

"Will it make my uncle angry?"

"Not if he doesn't know it was even part of the collection. I'm pretty certain he overlooked it."

She flashed a devious smile. "I would like it better if I knew it would piss him off."

"Why cause trouble when we don't have to? Will you do it?"

"I'm rich and bored. Causing trouble is about the only fun I have any more."

"Is it a deal?"

"You haven't told me what it is."

"Do we have a deal?"

"Sure," she said.

I looked at her standing over me in her skirt and open blouse and said, "And you get to keep your dignity."

She slid back on top of me. "Dignity is overrated." Emily kissed me until her hand moved across the blazer, feeling the box in my pocket.

"What's this?" she asked and sat up. Pulling it from my pocket, she opened the box and pulled out the brooch. "Quick, you're a naughty boy," she said and gave me a gentle slap on the cheek. "It's been right here all the time?"

She started to put it on, and I objected. "No, you can't wear that yet. You've got to keep it hidden until we can come up with a story for how you got it back."

She glared at me for a moment and then gave me a sinister laugh. She kneed me in the groin as she got up and said, "My house, my brooch, I'll do what I want."

"What about our deal?" I remained on the floor, holding my crotch and moaning.

"See yourself out, Mr. Quick."

From behind her, Frankie approached. He stopped, looked at me, then looked at Emily's unbuttoned blouse newly adorned with the brooch. He shook his head at both of us and said, "That thing is hideous."

Without another word, he disappeared again. Emily followed and I watched her departure from the floor.

11

———

I crawled on my hands and knees to the bag of baseballs. There was no honor among this group of thieves. I decided that any qualms I might have about acquiring the trophy through illicit means could be tossed out the window.

Time to pick up my balls and go home. Or at least go to the hotel. I started down one hall and then the next, assuming I would run into someone in this labyrinth eventually. I found Jeffrey, who seemed somewhat out of sorts.

"Did you wish to leave, sir?"

He seemed to be urging me more than asking me. That should have been a clue.

"Well, I was looking for the way out. Have you seen Zeus? Big fellow. Looks like he stepped out of a Bond movie? Unfortunately, he's my ride."

"He is in the library with Mr. Tarantola and a few

others. They are expecting you." He seemed to hesitate. "Should I show you the way out?"

I was confused by the question. "Do you mean show me to the study?"

"As I said, they are," he paused, "expecting you. Would you rather leave?"

This kind old man was throwing me a life preserver. Instead I chose to sink. "If they're expecting me, I suppose I should make my way to the library."

He sighed. "As you wish, sir."

I followed him down a wood-paneled corridor. We reached a double door and he opened it, revealing a large library. To the right were bookshelves two stories tall. Connected to them was one of those old-fashioned rolling ladders for access to the upper shelves.

On the left, a spiral staircase gave access to a loft area with more books. In the center was a sitting area with couches, chairs, and short bookshelves. Behind the sitting area was a desk. Seated behind the desk was Nick Tarantola. He watched as Zeus held Emily down and tried to take the brooch from her blouse. She resisted, shouting a few obscenities for good measure.

After a minute of squirming, she stopped him. "You're going to rip my blouse or break the clasp. Let go of me and I'll take it off."

He released her, and she took it off. Then she slammed it into his hand with the clasp open. He winced but didn't make a sound.

"Mr. Quick, I'm disappointed in you," Nick said.

"After our dinner conversation, I thought you were a man I could trust."

"I didn't give her the brooch, she took it from me."

"And yet you removed it from the rest of the merchandise to use as some sort of bargaining chip?"

I looked at Emily and she shrugged her shoulders. She may not be talking now, but she must have been blabbing up a storm before I got there.

"What can I say? She asked me to retrieve the brooch and I complied. The way I see it, I simply saved you the agony of watching her use that baseball bat to devalue even more of your collection. I'm sure that crystal piece she destroyed at dinner last night was worth a lot of money."

He considered my response. "You may have a point. But I doubt you did it out of loyalty to me and our family fortune." He looked at Emily and then back at me. "Normally, I would assume you were hoping to trade the brooch for a few moments of physical gratification—given the proclivities of my niece and the degenerate nature of men like you." I tried to let that one roll off.

He continued, "Yet she was just telling us that you were ready to turn down a carnal reward in exchange for a family heirloom for yourself." He rose and moved around the desk, stopping just inches from my face. "So tell me, Quick, what did you have in mind?"

I could deny that I made the offer, but I knew he

would see right through me. So, I lied. "The portrait of Chief Sockalexis."

He looked at Emily. "Is he telling the truth?"

"I told you when your goon was twisting my arm. He didn't actually tell me what the item was," she replied.

He looked back at me. "I'm inclined not to believe you. Seems like a silly thing to risk bodily harm over." He nodded his head towards someone behind me. I was so focused on Tarantola, I didn't realize Zeus had moved. He punched me in the back. I'm certain one of my kidneys exploded. It least that's what it felt like before I passed out.

When I woke up, the butler was applying a damp cloth to my forehead. "You've been unconscious, Mr. Quick."

"Really? I seem to remember being punched in the back." I tried to sit up, but the pain shot through my entire core.

"Mr. Tarantola says you probably fainted from heat exhaustion or dehydration."

"Do you believe that?"

"I believe people seem to faint a lot when Mr. Zeus is about," he answered.

I tried to sit up again, this time successfully. The pain wasn't much better, though. "I'm pretty sure Zeus tried to remove one of my organs with his bare hands. Do you see any blood back there?"

I pulled up my T-shirt and let him look. "No signs of

surgery, amateur or otherwise," he chuckled. "But there is considerable bruising."

"Are they done with me," I looked around. "Or, just waiting for me to wake up so they can continue the beatings?"

"The others have gone, sir. A car is waiting to take you to your hotel when you feel you can walk."

At this point, I realized I was stripped down to my underwear. My clothes were in a pile on the floor. "Did you take off my clothes?"

"They searched you sir. To see if you had taken anything else."

"Did they find anything?"

"No." He asked, "Should they have?"

"Not that I'm aware of. How about I get dressed?" I stood all the way up, and pain shot through my entire body. I leaned on Jeffrey for just a moment.

"Perhaps, you should rest a while longer?"

"No, I want to go home." I started to get dressed. "Did they leave me any instructions?"

"You are to await a call from Mr. Zeus, sir."

I finished getting dressed then he offered me a choice: a glass of water or a shot of whiskey. "I'll take the water."

I drank it in one gulp, then put down the glass. "On second thought, I'll have the whiskey."

"Of course, sir." He handed me the whiskey and I drank it in two gulps.

"Aah," I said. "Don't suppose I could get a double?"

He poured the drink and handed it to me. "Thank you," I took the glass and drank it in three gulps.

"Can I ask you a question?"

"Certainly sir."

"You seem like a decent guy. And if I'm not mistaken, you tried to warn me to leave instead of coming to the library."

He nodded. "Go on."

"You're savvy enough to know at least some of this family is friendly with organized crime. Has it always been this way?"

"For the most part, this family has been defined by service to mankind, industriousness, and class. Yet, they are not without their flaws. As with all great families, subsequent generations may not always share the same ideals as the ones before. Mr. Tarantola has long indulged dangerous appetites. However, I believe his connection with the Satellite group may be his down-fall. As a result, I fear this household will be brought to shame one day."

"You're very insightful," I replied.

I thanked him for his help, and we made our way to the car. Before I got in, he spoke softly. "You may have an eye for art, Mr. Quick. You may even fancy a portrait of a long-forgotten ballplayer. But your heart and soul are drawn to silver."

I looked at him and he allowed only the subtlest of grins. He knew I had lied to Tarantola. And he knew what I really wanted.

"Like I said, you're very insightful."

He continued, "Fifteen percent seems like a good number to keep me disinterested in the silver collection."

"Ten."

He thought for a moment. "Very well. I'll escort you to your ride."

WHEN I GOT BACK to the hotel, I called Simone. I wanted her to check on the baseballs and give me an update. She had also been checking my mail. I realize this is probably the dumbest thing I could have done—encouraging this girl when I really didn't want a relationship with her—but I was in a bind and needed help. She was eager to do it and Kevin was bartending until I could re-open the shop.

"Hi, Simone."

"Quick! How are you? When are you coming home?"

"I'll drive back in the morning. Did you check my mail today?"

"Yes, it's right here in front of me. Do you want me to open it and read it to you?"

"You brought my mail home?"

"No silly, I'm at your house."

"Oh, okay. Well, no need to read it to me. Before you leave there, could you check on the baseballs? Take a picture and text it to me."

"Sure, but I'm not leaving."

I had a sick feeling in my stomach. I wasn't sure whether it was her answer or the punch from Zeus. "Why not?"

"My place is a mess due to the police search, so I thought I would stay here until you get back. Then I thought you could help me clean up my place to pay me back for helping you out."

"Simone, why did the police search your house?"

"They were looking for stolen merchandise."

I cringed. "Why were they looking for stolen merchandise?"

"Oh, don't you worry. I stopped doing that when I turned eighteen. I haven't robbed anyone for at least seven years."

I didn't want to know any more. But I had to have more details. She was sitting in my living room. "Back up and start from the beginning. You used to rob people?"

"Just rich people. You know, the kind who have insurance. Me and my old boyfriend used to rob wealthy homes in Carmel. We stole fur coats, silver, that kind of stuff."

"And then what happened?"

"Well, we got caught. I was under eighteen, so I got juvie and my record is clean as a whistle now."

"And your boyfriend?"

"Ex-boyfriend. He's still in jail. He shanked a guard and they tacked on another ten years."

"So, why did they search your place?"

"The police said someone broke into a house and used the same MO that we did. They even left a pink skull, spray-painted on the wall, like I used to do. It was our calling card. Since I was the one not in jail, they assumed I was involved. Like I said, I haven't done anything since I turned eighteen. I was not going to spend my twenties in real jail."

"Oh, I remember the pink skull break-ins from the news. That was you?"

"That was me. Or us, I should say."

"How did you get caught?"

"Bobby—my ex—sold the loot to an undercover cop. They never would have caught us if not for that."

"Were you good at it?"

"Not something I'm proud of, but yes."

"If I needed to remove something from a mansion, could you show me how to do it and not get caught?"

"No, but I will come to Cleveland and get it for you."

12

―――――

When I got back to the hotel, I took a long shower and tried to take stock of my situation. Getting roughed up, Emily's betrayal, and being blackmailed had taken me to a dark place. I was considering three of my own scams while being forced to help Satellite carry out their own.

First, I had promised to help Valerie get the authentic Eddie Plank card. Then, I wanted to steal the Temple Cup. Next, I wanted to scuttle the sale of the Chief Sockalexis painting. It had been passed around undeserving hands long enough. Now it needed to go home.

Herman Trent was the anglicized name of a member of the Penobscot tribe. There is an ongoing debate about what his native name was, but it doesn't matter. What matters is that he painted and New Englanders paid him handsomely for his work. One painting for which he was not so handsomely compensated was his portrait of fellow Penobscot Louis Sockalexis. This portrait was supposed to hang in a place of honor at the Tribal Headquarters in Maine.

Instead, it was stolen and later forgotten by all but a few baseball artifact nerds (like me) and possibly a tribal historian. Then early one morning in June of 2009, the feds raided eight homes in Blanding, Utah (Don't feel bad, I had to look it up, too). It was the largest bust of archaeological and artifacts thieves in United States history. Operation Cerberus Action (FBI agents love Greek Mythology) netted 40,000 objects. Although most dated back hundreds and even thousands of years, one item that was inventoried was out of place. It was a painting of a 19th century baseball player. If the painting had been on the wall of any of those eight homes, the agents would have ignored it, never dreaming it had anything to do with the theft of Native American culture. But since it was in a crate with other more sought-after pieces, they figured it was stolen too.

At first, they called in an art appraiser to look at it. When he realized the subject of the portrait was a baseball player from the late 1800s, he felt someone from the memorabilia world ought to give an opinion. I never met this appraiser, but either he, or someone he knew, gave the FBI my name. So, I got on a plane to Salt Lake City.

And wouldn't you know it, when I got there, it was gone. One of the plaintiffs' attorneys had argued its inclusion into evidence was a mistake. He contended that the painting was clearly not an ancient artifact but a family heirloom. He also claimed that artwork by Herman Trent wasn't even hanging on the walls of any major museum (true). Hell, you couldn't even find him on Wikipedia (also true).

And some bent agent believed his story. Or was paid to believe it. Thus, the only portrait painted of Louis Sockalexis while he was alive passed illicitly into other hands. I raised a ruckus, but when the FBI finally agreed to ask for it back a few days later, the attorney claimed it was stolen out of his Lexus on the way home. How this portrait wound up in the Tarantola mansion was beyond my comprehension, but there it was.

How much was it worth? It depends on who you ask. The average art collector doesn't know Trent. But a degenerate collector with money would get off on the sordid provenance that came with this piece. And if that degenerate was also a Cleveland sports fan, well, add a zero (maybe two). But to the Penobscot Nation, it would be priceless.

So, convincing the Satellite crew to sell it publicly was my angle. Once it was listed for sale, I could tip off the tribe and the government would get involved. Then I figured the heat would be off me. Some days I'm so dumb you wonder how I breathe.

These things I pondered while standing in the shower, trying to relieve some of the pain from my last encounter with Zeus. I had one more thing to sort out:

how to switch out the fake baseball card Valerie purchased with the real one Satellite still had. I was putting her off. I had no idea how to get access to it before the auction. And waiting that long would be too late. Valerie would never agree to it.

My mind wandered, as it usually does in the shower. I thought about how I justified stealing the Temple Cup. Sure, it was stealing, but I was being forced to work for them against my will. I deserved compensation, didn't I? Any reasonable person would conclude the same thing, right? And that's when it hit me: Donnie would think the exact same thing.

My cell phone rang as soon as I got out of the shower. Valerie was angry. "Quick, I want that card or I'm going to the police. My buyer is getting impatient."

"I'll have it tomorrow."

"How?"

"Don't ask how. Just give me until tomorrow. I'll call you when I have it and we can arrange a place to meet."

"No tricks," she said. "And no more excuses."

"I promise, you will have the card."

"You better deliver this time." She hung up.

I had convinced her before my return to Cleveland to send me the card she had so I could switch it out. She kept her buyer waiting by claiming it was being photographed for an upcoming issue of *Smithsonian Magazine*. Valerie could be as deceitful as the rest of us dealers when she needed to be.

Next, I called Donnie and asked to meet him at his

hotel. He tried to get me to meet at a restaurant again, but I told him I wanted to talk where Zeus and the rest of Satellite wouldn't be watching or listening. Reluctantly, he agreed.

Early the next morning, I knocked on his door and he let me in, wearing a bathrobe and flip flops.

"Good morning."

"Why are we meeting this early, Quick?"

I asked, "No coffee yet?"

He shook his head. "What do you want?"

"I need the Plank."

"Yeah, I know. You want to switch out the fake with the real one when they do the auction. But that's not for a couple of weeks."

"No, I need it now."

"I can't help you then. Break into Satellite's warehouse and switch it yourself."

"I could do that. But then I would be trading a fake for a fake, wouldn't I?"

There's a reason I chose 6:30 in the morning to have this conversation. Donnie's not a morning person (neither am I). But Donnie's incapable of guile before 9 a.m. He shook his head and sighed. "How did you figure it out?"

"Human nature. I figured if I wanted to take something of value from these people in return for the inconvenience and abuse, then you probably were thinking of doing it, too. Or that you already had done it."

"They're smart, but they don't know this world as

well as you and me. It was easy to slip them one of the fakes and convince them it was the real deal. As soon as Zeus wasn't looking, I pocketed the real card. Of course, I had made an extra fake, so the count looked right to them."

"And how many fakes did they have you make? Surely, they didn't stop at just one. They're going to pass off more of these, aren't they?"

"You're starting to catch up, aren't you? Yeah, they had me make a dozen of each."

"Not cool that you held out on me," I said.

"I suppose I should say I'm sorry. But I'm not. I gotta take care of me. Which is why I'm not givin' you the card. Why should I? I need the money."

"Think of it as an investment. You do this for me, and I'll pay you back what the card is worth plus interest."

"The original card grades out to a PSA 4.5. I could easily get six figures for that."

"One hundred twenty thousand," I replied.

"You ain't got that kind of cash."

"Not on me. But if you help me out, that's what I'm offering for the card."

"How? You're not selling it to Valerie. You're trading her. Are you planning to sell her the fake?"

"Don't worry about the details. I'm offering to buy that card for $120K. I just need time to get the cash together."

"I don't think so. With your store being closed indefinitely, I just don't see how you can pay me back for a while."

I decided to play the best card in my deck. "I've got a T206 Wagner." His eyes perked up and I continued with only the important details as I saw them. "It's in a safe and when the dust settles on this, I'm going to sell it."

"And what's your commission on the sale?"

"It's not a commission sale. I own the card."

He smiled again. "Graded?"

"Not yet."

"What do ya think it will be graded at?"

I left out the fact that it was signed. "It's an eight or a nine."

He whistled and then muttered to himself. I could tell he was doing the math in his head. "You wouldn't lie to me would ya? You've got a Wagner?"

"Hand to God, I do."

He thought for a minute, then went to the closet and opened the hotel room safe. He brought out the Plank card and handed it to me. "I'm trusting you with my future."

"On my honor, I will pay you for this. And nobody will know you scammed Satellite."

"You mentioned if I wanted something of value from them, so would you. So, what are ya going to steal from them?"

"I was thinking about something shiny."

I LEFT Donnie's hotel and made my way to Valerie's. I called her en route. "I have the card."

"Are you sure it's the authentic one?"

"I would stake my reputation on it."

"Your reputation as a sports antiques expert or as a person?" she asked.

"Better go with the first one," I replied.

"Then I'll take it. How soon can you get here?"

"Pulling into the parking lot now."

"I'll meet you in the lobby."

"I can bring it to your room."

"I'll be down in a few minutes."

"Are you sure, I would be happy to spare you the trouble and come up there."

"I'm not decent yet."

"Neither am I," I replied.

"And that's why I'm meeting you in the lobby."

I found a comfy couch and began skimming a newspaper. Overhead, CNN was going on about a group called the Future Carnies of America. That sounded much more entertaining that what was in the New York Times, so I listened to the news. Apparently, some late-night comedian made fun of carnies. They got offended, tweeted something about his fans. The fans vowed to protest at carnivals across America. The Funnel Cake Fryer Manufacturers Association was deeply concerned about the negative impact this was going to have on their business. And I sat there thinking there is literally an association for everything.

"Good morning, Quick."

Valerie was wearing a mint green tank top, running shoes and black yoga pants with sheer cutouts.

"You're looking sporty."

"I'm either going to hit the treadmill or kick your ass," she said. She looked me over. "Depends on if you've been lying to me."

Can you believe the ingratitude? "Here's your card." I pulled it out of my shirt pocket, handed it to her and started to walk away.

"Quick, where are you going?"

I wheeled around, "I risked a lot getting you that card. Hell, I risked a lot even telling you the card you bought was a fake. And yet you still don't trust me. You still see me as one of them."

"One of who?"

"Them! The other dealers. The ones you look down on."

"Look, I really appreciate what you did. But what makes you different from all of them? They drink too much, they hit on anything in heels, and they are usually broke." She paused for effect, "Like you."

That hurt, but I leaned in close. "The difference is, none of *them* would have bothered. None of *them* would have risked their neck for you. And most importantly, none of *them* would have even known it was a fake."

"You didn't know it was a fake until Donnie told you."

"But I hadn't seen it yet, had I? I didn't hold it. I

didn't listen to its story," I said. "If I had, I would have known it was crap."

She laughed. "Listen to its story?"

"All genuine artifacts have a story. The fake ones have nothing to say."

"So, you're saying the cards and the balls and the jerseys talk to you?"

"The real ones do."

"I was wrong about you. You're not like the other people in this business. You're crazier."

I turned and walked away and kept going this time. Shouting back over my shoulder I said, "All artists and geniuses are a little crazy."

"You're neither," she replied.

13

————

I've always said, if you're going to commit a white-collar crime, do it in the place people least expect one to occur. Do it where people feel safe, secure, and in control. Do it in a place where people expect civility and class. In other words, do it in a museum. People who support and frequent museums have convinced themselves they are in an environment that is above the petty machinations of common criminals. It's a place where the patrons feel distanced from the stench of fraud. Poor deluded bastards.

The crew of Satellite, Cleveland Chapter, had picked an intriguing place to run this scam. The auction was being held in the Cleveland Museum of Art. Before I was allowed to go back to Indianapolis, I was told to meet Tarantola there to go over the details of the auction. When I arrived, he was waiting with Donnie, Zeus, and Mr. Newton.

They were listening to a museum official describe the facility. Newton introduced me. "Our late arriving friend is the poorly named Mr. Quick. He will serve as expert and historian on the baseball-related items to be sold at the auction. Mr. Quick, this is Truman Proudfoot, vice president of the museum board."

"It's an honor to meet you, Mr. Quick."

"I'm just happy to be here," I responded. Proudfoot missed the sarcasm, but Tarantola shot me a look. Quickly assessing the situation, I decided that Proudfoot was probably on the up-and-up and was just giving these men a tour. I played along and listened as he described the details of how the main hall would be set up, how they intended the traffic to flow, and where the catering team would set up and serve.

Only Newton spoke to our tour guide. The rest simply listened to the instructions without comment or question. Once the tour was over, Proudfoot left us to ourselves and Newton began giving orders. "Quick, I want you back here on Friday with those baseballs. You'll help our team and the Davis Group set up and then return to the Tarantola estate for a reception with some VIPs. Your job is to smile, answer baseball inquiries, and to dismiss any challenge to the authenticity of the items in this auction. I don't care if an item comes in looking like a third grader autographed it, you say it's legit. Get it?"

"And the day of the auction?" I asked.

"Same thing. You hang around. Answer questions

and make the buyers feel at ease with their purchases and the Davis Group at ease with their sales."

I asked, "And when we're done?"

"When the auction is done, you're free to go." I knew this was total crap but didn't argue. There are only two options with the mob. Either you continue doing illicit work for them or you discontinue breathing. Nobody is ever "free to go."

Newton gave Donnie a list of instructions, but I didn't pay attention. My mind wandered variously to the Temple Cup, Emily, Valerie, and Simone. I came back to the present in time to hear Newton tell us to get lost so he and Tarantola could talk. Zeus escorted Donnie and me outside, then returned to the museum.

"I hope I live through this. That money you owe me could help me start a new life," Donnie said.

I sat down on the steps of the museum and thought about our predicament. "It's not this job I'm so worried about, Donnie. It's what comes after."

"You don't think they'll let us go?"

"Would you? The way I figure it, they see us as either working for them, or we're loose ends."

"I reckon you're right, Quick."

"We can't just passively go along with this," I said. "Our only choice, Donnie, is to take these guys down. If not, we're going to be looking over our shoulders the rest of our lives."

"You mean go to the police? We're breaking laws here too, you know."

"Oh, no. Trust me, I don't want to go to the police any more that you do. No, what I have in mind is more complicated, but hopefully will get us in the clear."

"Whatcha got in mind, Quick?"

"Newton and Tarantola answer to somebody, right? There are people higher up the food chain watching them, just like they're watching us. What we have to do is crash this whole thing down around Newton and Tarantola. That way, they aren't coming after us because they're too worried about what their bosses are going to do to them."

"And how do you plan to do that?"

"I don't know yet."

"You're crazy, Quick."

"That's the second time I've been called that today."

"Because it's true." He got up to leave. "I'm not messing around with these guys, so leave me outta whatever it is you're doin'. And please don't get yourself killed before you get my money."

"I promise, you will get your money," I answered as he walked away in a huff. He didn't believe me.

But my plan was coming together. Proudfoot had to be a Native American name, I reasoned. If I could anonymously tip off the vice president of the museum that a stolen Native American artifact was being auctioned off at just the right time, I could scuttle the auction. If I could convince whoever was pulling the strings above Newton that this was an avoidable blunder on his part, then the heat would be on him, and Donnie and I could ride off into the sunset. However, I had to do all of this after the VIP party where I planned to have Simone steal the trophy. No problem, right?

And then Emily happened. When I reached my car, she called and asked me to meet her at a restaurant before I left town. I protested mightily. Really, I did. But she insisted she would make up for the previous day. Some men must suffer repeated humiliations on the path to wisdom.

And it's not like I didn't have fair warning that I was headed towards danger. Fate tried to intervene by having Ruben call me on the way to the restaurant.

My phone rang and before I could even say hello, he said, "So, did you sell that card yet?"

"No, I still can't get the safe open, but as soon as I do, I'm going to sell it and keep my word to my friend in Savannah."

"You know, I think all the trouble you've had is because you didn't sell it right away. God was watching."

"Oh, don't you start. I'm mixed up in something with a gangster who spouts Bible verses. He's got that televangelist vibe. I don't need it from you too."

"Did you say gangster?"

"Yeah, I'm in a deeper fix than the last time we talked."

"Why am I not surprised? Are there any women involved in this?"

"What do you mean involved?"

"You know what I mean, Quick."

"There are two women involved in this," I answered. "But not involved like the way you mean it."

"Only two?"

"Mainly two," I paused. "Maybe a third.

"When are you going to settle down and marry a nice Jewish girl?"

"Jewish? I'm not Jewish."

"This I know," he said. "But a nice Jewish girl would straighten you out. And you, of all people, need straightening out."

"Rainbow, I'll make you a promise. If none of these work out, I'll sign up for J-Date."

"What's that?"

"It's an online dating service for people of the Jewish persuasion."

"Again with the computer dating? Wasn't that how you met the girl who stole your 19th century catchers gear?"

"Yes, but you should have seen her the night before when she was wearing only the gear while we were ... never mind. I'm sure J-Date has a lot of nice Jewish girls who aren't memorabilia thieves.

"I don't understand you, Quick."

"What's there to understand? I gotta go. I'll call you in a couple of days," I said.

WHEN I GOT to the restaurant where Emily insisted we

meet, she was already seated at a table by a window. The sun was shining through and her silver dress shimmered for all to see. Have you ever studied a spider's web in the sunlight? Have you shifted your stance or tilted your head in order to catch the shimmer in its intricate pattern? You marvel at its beauty for a few seconds, then recall the horrible creature that constructed it. I'm not a fan of spiders. One bit me on the leg years ago and gave me an infection. I was about to be bitten by another here in Cleveland, with much worse consequences. And yet, here I was.

"Good afternoon, Quick." She extended her hand. I didn't shake it but sat down.

"I don't trust you," I began.

She retracted the hand without offense. Her reaction was more of a curiously surprised vibe. "You're not still angry about yesterday?"

"Shouldn't I be? You tricked me and then blabbed to your uncle. I think I have a bruised kidney."

"Well, I lost the brooch *and* I had to watch them beat you. It was very traumatic for me."

I was angry. I wanted to leave, but instead I took a drink of water and composed myself. "You said on the phone you had a business proposal. What's on your mind?"

She glanced down at her menu. "Can't we eat first?"

"Tell me what you have in mind and then I'll decide if I want to stay and eat."

She sighed and closed her menu. "Foreplay is not your thing, is it?"

"Stop. I'm not here because I'm turned on by you. I want to know why you would risk being roughed up yourself by your uncle's goons for meeting me. Is this for real or is it a trap?"

"I wanted my brooch and now I want that painting."

"Why the painting?"

"Because my uncle thinks it's worth a lot of money now that you risked the brooch for it. He thinks it could be the centerpiece of the auction."

"Your uncle is a moron."

"Is he? Maybe he is about a lot of things, but not this. You didn't get your ass kicked for something that was only going to fetch a thousand or two. You traded a jewel-encrusted brooch for it." She paused and laughed at my expense. "Or you would have, if I hadn't taken it."

Fine, let them think the painting is worth a fortune, I thought. But I was done. "If you want the painting or the brooch, then bid on them at the auction. I'm sure there's enough money in the trust fund." I stood up to leave.

"Oh, I intend to. That way my uncle will leave me alone. What I want you to do is lowball the appraisal on both. Then I want you to have Donnie Duluth paint a copy of the Sockalexis portrait. I'll keep the real one and sell the copy as an original for more money than I paid for it."

"Seriously? All of you are bent! So, you're part of Satellite too?"

"Keep it down. No, I'm not part of that mob, cult or whatever they are. This is my own deal. And it's between you, me, and Donnie."

"I'm not doing this. And I doubt Donnie will either."

"I'll pay $10,000 to each of you." She leaned back and flashed a wicked smile. "And I might even throw in a bonus for *you*."

"Stop, I said I wasn't turned on by you." I was lying.

She leaned forward. "You're lying."

"How do you know?"

"You're sitting here instead of in a car on your way back to Indianapolis. You could have done this over the phone, but you wanted to see me in person."

"This wasn't my idea," I said. Realizing I had raised my voice, I whispered, "You insisted we meet in person."

She continued to weave silk. "You could have refused. Don't deny it. I remember that look on your face when I first spoke to you."

Does the fly even feel it when he's been wrapped up? She gracefully brushed her hair back and leaned across the table. Walking her fingers up my arm, she said, "Just think about it. That's all I ask," she whispered. Then she stood and stepped beside me and gave me a soft peck on the cheek. So soft, I didn't even feel the fangs break the skin.

14

After my meeting with Emily, I left Cleveland in a brain fog. I don't even remember ordering food or eating. It had to be her venom, I decided later. In my impaired state, somewhere near Columbus, Ohio, I made the call to Donnie.

"How fast can you fake a painting?"

"What painting and how soon do you need it?"

"It's a portrait of Chief Sockalexis."

"The one from the Tarantola collection?"

"Yeah, that's the one. And I need it before the auction."

Donnie hung up. I waited until Dayton to call him back.

"Emily Tarantola wants us to do it."

"To scam her own family?"

"Sort of," I replied.

"I hate these people. I hate Cleveland. I hate baseball. I hate Satellite—whoever they are—and I'm starting to hate you."

"Don't be so dramatic. You don't hate baseball."

"I'm serious, Quick. Nothing about this feels right."

"Can you do it or not?"

"I can't fake a painting that fast. Paint it yes, but make it look as old as the original? That takes time."

"What if we don't need to show it aged by then? Just that it is being done."

"They are still going to want to see it finished eventually, right? The problem is the oil won't dry in time." He was silent for a moment and I didn't respond. I sensed he was already solving the problem in his head, even if he didn't really want to do it. He continued, "Unless I mix in some Liquin."

"What's Liquin?"

"It's a drying medium you can add to oil paints. You mix it in, then you paint in thinner layers than normal." He thought some more, "Oh, and if you paint the background in acrylic ..." More thinking. "And of course, you would need to hang it in a window with the back of the canvas facing outside."

"So, is it doable?"

"I don't know. I suppose I could make it dry to the touch, but it still wouldn't be completely dry for a month or two. Let me think about it."

He hung up again. I called him back just as I crossed the Indiana state line. "Well?"

"Well what?"

"Are you doing the painting or not?"

"You're going to get us killed."

"Yes or no? If not, I've got to find somebody else and I'm running out of time."

"I'll do it," he said.

"Great!" I asked, "Do you still hate Cleveland?"

He hung up on me again.

WHEN I PULLED up to my home, a man in a dark suit and sunglasses was leaving the porch. It wasn't Zeus, but he was built just like him and gave off the same vibe. By the time I got out of the car, he was already on the sidewalk. He didn't try to run or even walk at a hurried pace. It was more of a purposeful gait. I called after him as we walked away, but he didn't respond or even look back.

I took my suitcase out of the trunk and went to the front porch. There was a package by the door. It didn't appear to be opened or tampered with, but I had an uneasy feeling. It had a UPS label, but that clearly wasn't the UPS man who just left my property.

The box was light and just slightly bigger than a shoebox. Its return address was from Seattle. These were the baseballs from Victor. Was the goon in the suit checking out the box or the house? He wasn't looking for me, I thought, or he might have stuck around. I brought the box inside and set it on the kitchen counter.

Would Satellite check into the origin of this delivery, I wondered?

There was no sign of Simone when I went in, but the house seemed too clean. Was I indulging this girl too much? I didn't see a long-term future with her, but I did need her to help steal the trophy. Was that wrong? I decided to take a nap and see if my world was clearer when I woke up. It wasn't.

"Wake up, sleepy head."

Simone was lying next to me holding her phone above our heads. I groaned, "Don't take a picture of us."

"Too late," she said then kissed my cheek in time with the flash of her phone's camera. "That's going on Instagram."

"How long have I been asleep?"

"It's after seven. Want to go get some dinner?"

"No, I'll just grab something and get to work. I've got to finish the baseballs."

"If we're going to have a relationship, you have to be honest with me."

"What do you mean?"

"Like telling me you hired someone else to do the baseballs and not pretending you were doing them yourself."

"How did you know that? And I wasn't pretending for you. That was to fool these Satellite goons."

"Because I opened the package on the kitchen counter."

"Okay, if we're going to have a relationship"—I can't

believe that came out of my mouth—"you've got to stop opening my mail and my packages."

"So, you admit we're in a relationship?"

Dammit! How do I get tangled in these webs? "No!" She looked crushed. "Well, maybe." Simone brightened. "I don't know. This is all going so fast and I'm under a lot of pressure right now. The fire, the blackmail, the auction coming up. It's too much."

"Another reason why you can't do without me. Anyway, I figured it out when I saw what was in the box." She propped up on one elbow. "And don't take this the wrong way, but they look way better than yours. I'm no expert, obviously, but side by side, there's no comparison."

"You think they will figure it out?"

"Not as long as they don't see them together. I think your plan," she paused, "if I understand it correctly, is pretty sound."

"There was a man on the porch when I got home. Dressed in a dark suit and sunglasses. Buzz cut, dark brown hair. Did you see anybody like that lurking around while I was away?"

"No, that doesn't ring a bell, but I'll be on the lookout."

AFTER DINNER, we went out onto the porch and sat in the swing with the lights off.

"So, what is it you want me to steal in Cleveland?"

"It's a trophy made of silver. About 30 inches high. There are two pieces, unattached. The top part is the silver trophy itself. It is wide at the bottom and tapered towards the top with two ornate handles. On the front, a baseball player extends the length of the neck and an inscription on the lower two-thirds reads, 'The National League of Professional Baseball Clubs.' The trophy rests on a black base with a silver engraved plate."

She smirked, "So, I won't be able to tuck it into my bra?"

I paused and looked at her chest. "No, probably not." She punched my arm and I continued. "Our one chance is during the reception the night before the auction. I know there will be caterers to supplement the house staff, so maybe you could blend in with them?"

I let her think quietly for a minute or two and she responded, "I like the idea of doing this during the party. People will be distracted, and the external alarm won't be turned on."

"The trophy is in a glass case with other silver items. Try not to give into the temptation to help yourself to any of the others."

She elbowed me in the ribs. "I'm not a criminal. Well, maybe I am. But I'm only doing this for you, so don't get all high and mighty, Mr. Baseball Forger."

"My apologies." I continued, "When you're facing the cabinet, it's on the lower left side behind a silver platter on a stand. You'll have to move the platter to get to the trophy but be sure to place it back in the same spot. If this is done right, it might be years before anyone knows it's missing. Maybe never. I get the sense only the mansion staff remembers it's even there."

"Does the case have an alarm? Are there any cameras in those rooms?"

"Not that I'm aware of. It does have a lock, and the butler keeps the key. I'm guessing based on your past, we're not going to need it. Is that a fair assumption?"

"I'll handle the lock." She snuggled in closer. "Does it turn you on that I was once a criminal? Do you like bad girls?" The question surprised me, considering the elbow I took a few minutes earlier.

"I will be turned on when I get back to Indy and find you holding that trophy."

"I'm not going back without you," she said.

"Oh, yes you are. We can't stay in the same hotel or even ride up together. It's too dangerous. Once you get that trophy, you head back here and go to your place. If they do figure out it has been stolen, they will search me and my hotel or my house before looking elsewhere. You and the trophy stay away until I say it's safe."

"How long will that be?"

"I'm hoping just for a few days. Maybe a week."

"I don't like it," she said. "But I suppose I'll go along. You're going to make it up to me."

"Of course, I'll make it up to you."

She stood up from the porch swing and tugged my arm. "Starting right now." The house was dark, but light from the street gave us enough illumination to navigate the living room. I went willingly to the couch where she pushed me down and climbed on top of me. I should have resisted. I should have kept trying to slow things down between us. At the very least, I should have locked the door.

Simone took off her shirt and tossed it behind her head. A second later, it came back, grazing her hair and hitting me in the face.

"Put your shirt back on, Miss." The lights went on. "Good evening, Mr. Quick." The man in the suit was back.

15

———

"**I**f this is about becoming a Mormon, you should know I've already been rejected." I shook my head. "I couldn't give up caffeine."

He didn't find it funny. "I'm here for the balls." He pointed towards the counter with a gun he held in his left hand.

"Those balls?" I asked. "Those belong to Satellite."

He flashed a smile, "No shit. And they sent me to collect them."

"Why? Don't they believe I'll bring them to Cleveland?"

"Oh, they're sure you're coming to Cleveland. They just think you'll bring the shitty balls you created and not the ones made by our friend in Seattle."

My heart went into my stomach. They knew about Vic. Was he working for them? Or did I just accidentally bring him into this mess? I was terrified. The man in the suit walked to the counter where Simone had opened the box and lined them up. He inspected them for a few moments. "You didn't think you were fooling anybody with the ones you were making?"

Simone glared at me and said, "I told you so."

I told her, "Put your shirt on."

I looked at him. "I was just trying to learn the craft and buy myself some time. I had no intention of trying to pass mine off in the auction."

"Oh yeah? Well, you can explain all that to the boss when you get there. I'm taking these, and this doesn't change anything. You're still expected in Cleveland. You're still expected to follow the same routine." He carefully replaced each of the baseballs into the box. I didn't even get a chance to inspect them.

I had a thousand questions but was too afraid to ask. How long had he been listening? Did he hear our plan to steal the Temple Cup? Was he in cahoots with Vic? And most importantly, why would I think of the word cahoots when I never actually say the word cahoots? My mind was overloaded.

The best I could come up with was, "How did you get in my house?"

He pointed at the door and shot me a look that implied he was waiting for the next stupid question. "I'm leaving now. I'll assume that since you haven't left the couch and she is still sitting there in her bra that you're not dumb enough to try to stop me."

I nodded. "So, what now?"

He eyed Simone, who still hadn't put her shirt on. "You go back to doing what you were doing." Then he looked at me. "I go back to Cleveland."

Out the door he went, and I got up to lock it behind him. It felt stupid and futile.

Simone watched me pace but didn't speak. I had to decide what to do about Victor. How did they know? Was my house bugged? If Vic was in on it, calling him would make it worse. If he wasn't, I had to warn him of the danger he faced. There were no good choices. I decided to sleep on it, though I tossed and turned most of the night. Simone stayed despite the mood-killing trajectory the night had taken.

The next morning, I woke up to the phone ringing. I hoped it was Vic, saving me the trouble of calling. Although, that wasn't likely, considering the time difference from Seattle to Indianapolis.

"I found somebody to open the safe."

It was Kevin on the line. I had forgotten about my other dilemma. I had tasked him to find a trustworthy person to get inside my melted safe so I could retrieve the priceless baseball card. Funny how threats to your life and well-being can sort of push a fortune out of your head.

I told him that I couldn't pay him back right away for his time, but to keep track of it and I would compensate him. He probably would have done it for free. Every true collector longs to see the T206 Wagner up close. Kevin was practically giddy when I asked him to do it.

"That's great. Can you schedule for after the weekend? I need to go back to Cleveland one last time. I want to be there when he opens it."

"Sure, no problem. One thing, though. I found a news story online from Channel 7 in Denver. They tested several fire safes to see if they actually worked."

"Why do I think I'm not going to like this?"

"The model you own didn't do so well. The lock melted and there was water damage to the inside."

"How long did they let it burn?"

"Thirty minutes."

"How long did the firefighters say my fire lasted?"

"Forty-five."

"Well, the card was in a top loader, so there is hope. As long as it didn't get so hot the plastic melted around it." A top loader is a plastic protector for cards. They are great for modest price cards, but a truly expensive one needs to be slabbed. And that's usually after it is appraised, which would have been my next step if I had any luck or brains. Like I said, sometimes I'm dumber than dirt.

"Keep thinking positive. And don't Google that video. You'll want to kill yourself."

"If it's that bad, why did you tell me about it?" I hung up.

Can you believe that? Here I am keeping him gainfully employed (more or less) while my store is ungainfully closed, and he's bringing me down with negative talk. People are the worst.

After a shower, I made breakfast for us. I thought full-stomach Simone would be easier to let down than "hangry" Simone. I was wrong.

"What do you mean I can't go?"

"They know! We can't do it now."

"Don't you dare cut me out of this now. I'm going. Even if you tell me I can't go, I'm still going to drive to Cleveland and steal that trophy."

I felt genuinely worried for Simone. Maybe I cared about her more than I had let myself believe. "Look, I've seen what they do to people. It was a bad idea from the beginning. I should have never asked you to do it."

She got up in my face. "I'm going."

"No, you're not."

She threw her fork on the ground. "Yes, I am."

"No, you can't go."

She threw her napkin in my face.

"Don't be ridiculous."

"You're not going, Simone!"

While keeping eye contact with me, she threw her plate at the sink. But instead of shattering against the stainless steel, it sailed right out the small window above the faucet.

The lack of dramatic noise caused her to look at the sink. "Where did that go?" she asked.

"All the way to Cleveland," I answered.

She stared at the window, then turned back to me.

Her voice softened. "I don't think he heard us. We weren't talking loudly, and there isn't any place he could have been hiding in your front yard. He must have been waiting in a parked car and watched us get up and go in."

"Yeah, but they knew about the baseballs. They're listening to us somehow."

"I think you're being paranoid."

"I *am* being paranoid. And with good reason! We're calling it off."

"Calm down. If he heard us planning it, he would have threatened us. He was completely focused on the baseballs."

"Maybe. I just don't want you to get hurt."

"That's sweet, but I'm a big girl and can handle myself. Besides there was always a possibility of that anyway."

At this point, I should have dug in my heels and said no. All she had left to throw was a cup of milk, and it was plastic. But my plate still had some scrambled eggs on it. And there was a butter knife on the table. So, I pulled my food and utensils closer to me and acquiesced.

"Since you're going to do this, there is one thing extra I would like you to do."

This intrigued her. "Anything! What do you want me to do?"

"You mentioned you left a calling card when you were breaking into houses as a teenager."

"Sure, the pink skull. Do you want me to paint a pink skull in the showcase? I don't think there will be time."

"No, I want you to leave a baseball card instead."

"A baseball card?"

I got up from the table and said, "I'll be right back." I returned and handed her the card. It was a 1989 Fleer Billy Ripken. Actually, it was a reproduction of that particular card. I had a few hundred of them printed up as a joke.

"Why would you want me to leave this?"

"Take a close look at the bottom of the bat."

"Oh my gosh," she shouted. "are you serious? They didn't really print this did they?"

"Yes they did," I told her. "It was an error at the factory. Somebody played a prank on Ripken and wrote an obscenity on the bottom of his bat the day the baseball card pictures were taken. The card company didn't catch it in time and some of them made it do stores."

"Is it valuable?"

"An original can fetch $50 on up, depending on quality. But there are lots of fakes out there. Like the one you're holding."

"And you want me to leave this card with an F-bomb on it where the Cup is sitting now."

"Yes, I do." I kissed her on the forehead. "Yes, I do."

SIMONE LEFT after I finished breakfast and I went to

work on the provenance of the Temple Cup. I knew the original was located at the National Baseball Hall of Fame in Cooperstown, New York. So, I called a friend at the research library and asked him to inspect the Cup for a maker's mark or inscription that told who minted it.

Two hours later, I had my answer: The Allegheny Silver Company of Pittsburgh. More research on the web revealed the name of the owner and the fact that the company had closed not long before World War II. I tracked down a couple of descendants and got a voice-mail for the first. After leaving a message, I called another family member. She was helpful but must not get a lot of calls. For two hours, she talked my ear off. She was well versed in the family history, but not so much about a trophy that had to do with baseball. She did, however, have one useful nugget—the name and descendants of the guy who did most of the casting. Apparently, his son and her grandmother were married for a while. From there, she spent an hour explaining to me the intricacies of their meandering family tree.

Once I finally extracted myself from her genealogy lecture, I called the grandson of the trophy maker. He was hard of hearing, so I practically had to shout.

"Do you remember your grandfather ever mentioning a baseball-related trophy?"

"You mean the Temple Cups?"

"Yes, that's it. But there was just one of them."

"No, as I recall there were four."

"Four?"

"Yes, each of the team's owners who won the championship didn't want to give the trophy back, but that was the deal. So, they got in touch with my grandfather to make a copy. Crooked bunch, the lot of them."

"But your grandfather made the trophies."

"Well sure, he wasn't going to pass up an easy buck. So, he charged them double what he charged for the original just to keep his mouth shut. Hell, even the Allegheny Silver Company didn't know he made three more of them."

"So, is the one in the Hall of Fame the original?"

"Beats me. There is one way to tell, though."

"Yeah, how's that?"

"The original has his initials on the inside just under the lip. The letters 'D' and 'N' for Dimitri Neal. Find the D and the N, and you've found the real Cup."

"That's good to know. Thank you."

"I'm assuming since we're having this conversation, one of the others has turned up." The old guy was smart. "Wealthy families, like the kind that own baseball teams, have secrets, Mr. Quick. Some are worth knowing. And some are a dangerous burden to know. Do you follow me?"

"Not really."

"My grandfather traded the money for keeping the secret of four very narcissistic and wealthy men. It made him paranoid. The poor man was looking over his shoulder the rest of his life. Just something to think about before you buy one of them."

"I'll keep that in mind."

"I know you won't, but thanks for indulging an old man. Good luck, Mr. Quick."

I thanked him and hung up. So, there were three copies and none of them had surfaced over the years. That likely meant they hadn't survived or had long been forgotten like the one in the Tarantola house. Even with three copies, they could still command a good price at auction. Better yet, if the one in the Hall of Fame was a copy, and one of the three in private hands was real, then the price would go up. If the three owners would go to the lengths of having a copy made, who could say one of them didn't keep the original when it was time to change hands?

It was almost 10 p.m., and I wanted to get an early start on the road, so I got ready for bed. The silver-smith's grandson's words played over and over in my head as I brushed my teeth. "... looking over his shoulder the rest of his life."

Then the phone rang once more. This time it was Vic. "You didn't tell me those baseballs were for Satellite."

"You didn't ask, and I didn't think it mattered," I responded. "Look, I'm sorry if I got you in trouble. They're going to be leaning on you now to work for them."

He laughed. "Quick, I already do."

I felt a chill run down my spine and for a moment I couldn't breathe. "I don't understand."

"They asked you to do those baseballs because they thought they might be able to find a cheaper source than me. Hell, this doesn't hurt me, it only makes my position with them stronger. They're about to launch a major autograph counterfeiting operation in Seattle, and I'm going to be rich. You on the other hand, have little to offer them after Cleveland. I would be worried if I were you."

"And to think I was concerned about you."

"I like you, Quick. But I warned you not to go down this path."

"I've got to go, Vic. I think I'm going to be sick."

"Good luck, Quick."

It seemed every time I thought I was being careful or smart, I was neither. Careful and smart at this point would have been going to the police. But why change direction now? Victor, Satellite and the Tarantolas had taken up too much of my life the past few weeks. I was ready to be done with all of them. Time to go to Cleveland and get this over with.

16

I got up at four o'clock the next morning and managed to be on the road by 4:30. There is no appropriate amount of caffeine that can fix being on the road that early. I don't think my brain fully engaged until I got to the Ohio border. During a stretch where I-70 was down to one lane, I'm pretty sure I saw the Grim Reaper between two orange barrels next to the highway. His scythe was leaning against the guard rail and he was drinking a Starbucks. I pulled off at the next exit and got more coffee.

My phone rang as soon as I got to the Cleveland city limit. It creeped me out. How closely were these people watching me? Did they have some sort of GPS bug on my car?

"Proceed to the Cleveland Museum and ask for Madge."

"Zeus, ole buddy! I missed you too! How are you this fine morning?"

"Go straight to the museum," he said with no emotion.

"Will you be there when I arrive? What are you wearing?"

He hung up. It must be miserable going through life without a sense of humor.

THE CLEVELAND MUSEUM OF ART was full of activity. Buses moved in relentless formation, dispensing children, teachers and chaperones. Tour guides met them and firmly but politely shared the agenda, rules and warnings about misbehavior. I could see another line of vehicles (white box trucks with no markings) driving around to the back of the museum.

I entered and went to the information desk. A smiling but harried employee with a nametag that said Blake greeted me. "Good morning. May I help you?"

"I'm here to see Madge."

He looked me up and down. Apparently, I didn't look like the kind of person who normally asks for Madge. "Are you sure? She works in the back."

I could see there were two classes of employees at the museum: the front-facing purveyors of art and class and the people who "work in the back."

"Yes, I'm sure that's the name I was given."

He paused, looked me up and down again and said, "I'll call her."

I looked around the expansive lobby, taking in the kids and the chaos. I noticed a man walk in who glanced at me, then casually moved towards the gift shop. Too casually. It was the same man I had seen talking to Valerie's boyfriend at the hotel.

"She'll be out in a minute, sir. In the meantime, have a seat on our newest waiting benches." He had temporarily forgotten I might be a "work in the back" kind of guy and grabbed my arm. With all the drama of a gender reveal, he said, "They were designed by the anarchist poet, Splatter. Aren't they gorgeous?"

I turned and didn't see a bench. Instead, I saw a child sitting on a stack of clear boxes. I was about to ask if the benches were behind the boxes when my brain registered what he had just said.

"His name is Splatter?"

"Their name," I was corrected with just a hint of disdain.

"Splatter is a group?"

My ignorance had touched a nerve. "Splatter is non-binary, non-gender conforming. Splatter's preferred pronouns are they and them."

I turned back and realized the boxes were the bench. It was made entirely of clear containers filled with what looked like Chex Mix. The containers were glued together to form the bench. Sitting on the bench, the little boy who had escaped from his school group was opening the containers and sneaking out bites. From his angle, Blake couldn't see that the art was being consumed.

"Is that Chex Mix," I asked.

Blake answered enthusiastically, "Yes, isn't it glorious? Splatter is in a snack and cereal phase right now." He looked both ways and lowered his voice. "Rumor has it, Splatter's next piece is a reimagining of Mount Rushmore only with cool people like Lady Gaga and Obama." He paused and looked around. "And it's made of jellies and jams." He was shivering with excitement. Splatter has that effect on people. Apparently.

"And it's coming to this museum?"

He nodded, then shrieked, "Little boy! Stop eating the waiting bench!" Blake looked at me and shook his head. "I hate Cleveland Public Schools days."

I gave him a sympathetic nod and wandered over to the bench. Before I could ask the boy to sneak me some pretzels, Blake made his way around the bench and admonished the child again. I wanted to intervene on his behalf, but Madge arrived.

"You Quick?"

"You Madge?"

"Who else would I be?" Madge was mid- to late fifties, judging by her gray hair and weathered face. She was thick and wore grey work pants, a grey work shirt with a sewn-on name tag (which was blank) and black boots. She looked all business, not even taking a second to notice the chaos of the public school kids, the shrieking of Blake, or the snack food furniture.

I followed her past the screaming throngs of school children and through a door marked "staff only."

We proceeded to a dock where trucks were unloading. She told me to wait and shouted instructions to warehouse workers, truck drivers and even security guards. Nobody talked back to Madge. They just nodded, said okay, and carried out her instructions.

When she finished, she pointed to a cart with a wooden crate on it and told me to follow her with it. We proceeded along another hallway until we came to a large hall. Donnie was already there and I noticed her tone got just slightly softer as she continued to bark out orders.

In the center were rows of chairs, enough to accommodate 200 viewers. A phone bank was being set up on tables in the back by Davis Group employees. The phone tables faced a stage with a podium and tables to each side. Down the right and left side of the room, the tables were being loaded with merchandise. Hanging on each wall were giant tapestries. Some hung almost to the floor and covered recesses hidden along the east wall.

Madge instructed the other workers to leave and attend to another project. Then she addressed me and Donnie. To me she said, "You continue to bring any box marked with a green dot up the same way we came and to this room. Open each one and set the contents on this table." She looked at Donnie and cracked the slightest smile and pointed to him, "He will group like items together after you deliver them. Don't worry too much about the arrangement now, just get it all out and organized and the Davis Group people will take it from there."

Donnie and I looked at each other. "Any questions?" she asked.

I shook my head no and headed for the loading dock. When I got back with my first load, neither Donnie nor Madge were around. I thought it was odd, but I kept working. After about 45 minutes, I had filled the tables on the west wall. So, the next trip, I pushed the cart to opposite side of the room with the longer tapestries. That's when I heard a bit of a commotion.

Looking at the gap between the tapestries and the floor, I could see a pair of black boots attached to legs wearing gray pants that were walking briskly towards the door on the south side of the room. Then Donnie emerged from one of the recesses behind the tapestries.

It all made sense. Donnie being here already. The change in Madge's tone, that little smile she cracked. "Donnie, did you just have sex?"

"What are you talking about?"

"Your zipper is undone. Your belt is undone. Your hair is messed up."

"Yeah, so I've been working."

"And Madge just scurried the other way, like she didn't want to be seen."

"Yeah, so?"

"It looks like you're sweating."

"So, I sweat when I'm hump... I mean when I'm hanging pictures."

"Hanging pictures?" I laughed. "Is that what you call it?"

He turned red. "Go on, Quick. I'm scared out of my mind. I needed something to take the edge off."

"In a museum?" I looked around. "That's one step away from doing it in a church." Donnie crossed himself. "I didn't know you were Catholic. You, the master forger?"

"I may be a forger, but I go to confession."

"Does that make it any better?"

"Gets me to sleep at night. Besides, I think the priest gets tired of hearing about all those everyday sins. Seems to me he wants to hear about a forgery now and again. In a way, I'm doing the good Lord a favor by keeping His man from getting bored with his work." He paused and thought for a moment. "Yeah, that's right. Me being a criminal is, in a way, doing the Lord's work."

"That's a hell of a way to look at it, Donnie."

"Don't talk like that, we're in a church," he replied.

"Museum."

"Museum, church. Whatever. Seems you could be a little more respectful."

"You just had sex behind some tapestries."

He stared at me in silence for a few awkward moments. "I'm going to get something to drink."

"Bring me back a water," I answered.

Considering Vic had turned out to be on Satellite's team, I had to consider whether Donnie was playing me. But after a giving it some thought, I decided he was just horny and Madge was just an employee of the museum and not connected with Satellite. Otherwise, Donnie wouldn't have indulged in whatever went on in that dark little alcove. I took my cart and went for another load.

That's when I saw Proudfoot and decided this was my chance. He was coming out of the men's room when I spotted him. I looked both ways for signs of Zeus or any other members of Satellite. Convinced that it was clear, I asked him to step back inside the bathroom and spilled my guts.

"It's about this auction. There's an artifact in it that has significant meaning to your people."

"My people?"

"Indian. I mean Native American."

"What tribe?"

"Penobscot."

"I'm Chippewa."

"Same difference."

"Not same difference. And kind of racist."

"Look, I don't have time to be culturally sensitive. I'm scared to death, and I'm being forced to do stuff I don't want to do. Do you care about this painting or not?"

He stared at me for a moment, then nodded. "Okay, go ahead."

I told him about the painting of Sockalexis but left out Emily's plan altogether. I'm not really sure why, but I was sure her poison was still in my system. "And what do you want me to do," Proudfoot said. "Go to the police?"

"No, not the real police. But isn't there some tribal Indian artifact police that could step in and stop the sale?"

"Tribal Indian artifact police," he asked. I shook my head yes. "Are you out of your mind?" I shook my head no. "Yeah, there's a tribal Indian Artifact police. They're kind of busy now though. They're trying to solve a land deal that went bad a few hundred years ago. Maybe you heard of that crime?" I didn't shake my head at all.

He continued, "This falls under the National Park Service jurisdiction. I'll have a chat with them."

"National Park Service," I said. "Who would have thought."

He looked at me like I was an idiot. "Yeah, who would have thought." Some days I'm dumber than dirt.

I made my way back to the hall with the merchandise. Donnie was displaying several works of art that had nothing to do with baseball or the Cleveland Spiders. In fact, as I stood and took in everything around me, it seemed like there was more art than baseball artifacts.

"Donnie, where is all the baseball stuff?"

"A lot of it is still at the Tarantolas' house for the reception. It will be brought over in the morning."

"I guess I just assumed this was all about baseball."

"No, it's all about fraud."

I looked around the room. "At least two-thirds of it is going to be legit."

He laughed, "More like ten percent." He lowered his voice, motioned for me to sit down and then cleared his voice. "I've been holding out on you, Quick."

"How so?"

"Most of this art is fake. Even though the museum curator and most of the so-called experts think it's real," he said.

"How's that possible?"

"When I said they dangled something related to forged art to me after this was over, I lied. We've been faking provenance on all these paintings for the past three years. I wasn't lying when I said I don't want to work for them anymore."

"What do you mean you've been faking the provenance?"

"We have a guy who goes to their archives for research on a regular basis. All this time he's been slipping in ownership histories of fake paintings. Then when a painting shows up for sale or to be loaned to the museum, voilà! There's a document down in the basement that conveniently proves it's real."

"Not sure I'm following you."

"Okay, take Picasso for example. We forge a 'forgotten' Picasso painting of a turtle. Then we invent a history of ownership and print that onto yellowed old paper. Slip into the museum archives, slide the fake history into the records. Then we show up with the painting, the curators say I've never heard of a Picasso painting of a turtle. We say, no? How about we check the archives? And wouldn't you know it, the archives contain the history of Picasso's long forgotten turtle."

I looked around the room, "You didn't really pass off a Picasso turtle painting, did you?"

"No, of course not. You don't fake the artists that have entire college courses devoted to them. You do other famous artists—second or third tier down from the Picassos of the world. That way it's more believable that one or two of their paintings could have slipped through the cracks. And of course, this 100-year-old museum has documentation!"

"Forged documentation."

"Exactly."

"To pull this off," I asked, "wouldn't Satellite have to have a mole in the museum?" I didn't get an answer.

"Donnie," Madge called out. "My staff will finish the rest. "You boys are supposed to head over to the Tarantolas for the fancy shindig over there."

"I'll see you later," Donnie said.

"Wait," I whispered. "Why tell me about the paintings?"

"So, you know how deep I'm in this. And how dangerous it is for me to be helping you and Tarantola's crazy niece. I'm scared, Quick. I don't want to die, and I don't want to go back to jail."

This new complication was all I could think about as I drove to the hotel. A quick shower and change of clothes and I was ready to go to the reception. I wanted to call Simone and tell her to stay away, but I was afraid I was being watched. Or worse, that my calls were being listened to by Satellite. In my heart, I wanted that trophy. But my head wanted Simone safe in Indianapolis.

WHEN I ARRIVED at the Tarantola mansion, I felt like my suit was about $1,000 too cheap for the occasion. Even the butler who ushered me in looked at it sideways. But it was Frankie who was offended the most.

"That suit is hideous."

I looked at myself in the hallway mirror. "Frankie, is everything hideous to you?"

He looked me up and down. "Did I offend you?"

"A little bit."

"Well, then I'm glad I didn't tell you that your suit looks like it came out of Al Bundy's closet."

"You've been a delightful greeter, Frankie." I started to walk away.

"If it cheers you up, you look better than the Indian." He kept talking, but I ignored him. I should have paid more attention.

The butler walked me to the banquet room where staff were making last-minute preparations. As catering folks went this way and that, I looked for Simone. Zeus told me to hang by the merchandise along a side wall and answer questions.

Once the guests arrived, I engaged with a variety of collectors and assured them that the items were of the highest quality and value. Some of them really were and I hoped they would go to good homes. Time slipped by quickly and still no sign of Simone. As the evening started to wrap up and the crowd thinned, it was easy to scan the room. But I saw no hint of the roller-skating master thief.

Finally, Newton and Zeus arrived and asked me to follow them. They took me to a parlor, and we waited in silence. Well, they waited in silence.

"Did either of you taste those things that were wrapped in bacon? Don't know what they're called but I must have snagged a half dozen of them."

No response.

"They did make me thirsty though. And the champagne guy was not covering each side of the room equally. He only made one pass to where I was at the whole time."

No response.

"Have either of you guys ..." I was cut off.

"Enough, Mr. Quick. We will have a word with you now in my library. I think you have fond memories of the place," Nick Tarantola said behind me.

I turned to see him standing there with Proudfoot. Frankie was right, my suit did look better. It was little consolation, however, and my heart sank into my stomach. "I thought a Cherokee would have more honor."

"Chippewa," he said.

"Same differ..."—he hit me in the ribs before I could utter what was clearly an inappropriate response.

"Let's go." Tarantola directed Zeus to hold my arm and we made our way down a long hallway towards the library. As we went, we passed a blond staff member pushing a large rolling cart in the opposite direction. Nobody even looked at her.

17

"So, you're the mole," I said to Proudfoot.

"Excuse me?"

"The mole in the museum who's helping Satellite." I realized I could be exposing Donnie to some trouble if they understood how much I knew, so I didn't mention the forged documents and fake paintings. "I assumed there had to be someone there who was in on it. Didn't figure it to be you."

"Well, on behalf of Satellite, and all Native Americans," he grinned, "I thank you for speaking up."

"I don't suppose that's going to win me any points, is it?"

He looked at Tarantola, who shook his head solemnly. "No, probably not," he answered.

Without warning, Zeus punched me in the stomach. I retched a little on Proudfoot's shoe. He shoved me to the floor and pulled the handkerchief from his suit pocket. "You're not worth what these shoes cost."

"Pretty fancy on your salary." I had no idea if they were fancy or not, of course. He could buy his shoes at Target and I wouldn't know the difference. Of course, Frankie wasn't a fan of his ensemble.

"Satellite has been good to me," Proudfoot answered. "And for letting them know your thoughts about the Sockalexis painting, I'm sure they will take care of me again."

He looked at Tarantola, who smiled and looked down at me on the floor. "Of course, we will. Now, you get a good night's sleep for the auction tomorrow and we'll take care of Mr. Quick."

He followed Proudfoot to the door, said something to him I couldn't hear and they both laughed. Then he shut the door and returned to the problem at hand: me. While he tried to sort that out, I remained on the floor. Too tired to fight at the moment. Too exasperated that all my plans kept falling apart. Too worried about Simone.

"I'm not going to kill you," he finally said.

"Well, that's a relief," I answered. "I'll just dust myself off and head back to the party."

"I'm not going to promise you're going to get out of this alive, but that depends on your behavior. What I am going to tell you is that Apollo is going to go visit your lady friend in Indianapolis, should we decide we aren't happy with your cooperation over the next 24 hours."

"Who's Apollo?"

"I believe you met him in Indianapolis. He retrieved the baseballs."

I looked at Zeus. "Brother of yours or just a creepy coincidence?"

Zeus didn't answer. Tarantola continued, "Now take off your clothes, Mr. Quick."

I looked at him and then at Zeus. Then back and forth at both. "You know it's really getting late," I said. "I should get a good night's sleep for the auction too."

Zeus drew a gun. "Take off your clothes."

"Guys, I'm pretty sure I'm not into whatever you're going to suggest next, so can we call it a night?"

Tarantola continued, "Apollo sent word that he is convinced you're planning to steal something. I need to be convinced that you're not. So, take off your clothes."

"All of them or just my pants and shirt?"

"All of them," he answered. "You tried to get the brooch to Emily. Who knows what you might be hiding in a body cavity?"

"You're kidding right?"

Zeus and Tarantola just stared back. I angrily took off my clothes and threw them on the floor. Zeus produced a metal detector from a black duffel bag, just like the wands at airport security. Who the hell has one of those handy? It was humiliating. But Zeus was just getting started.

"Can I smack him around some, boss?"

"Not so much he can't work tomorrow," he replied and left us alone.

Something about being naked makes it infinitely harder to fight someone. You feel completely vulnerable, even if the person you are fighting is smaller than you. But in this case, Zeus was taller, stronger, and in better shape. And he was clothed.

He took off his jacket and rolled up his sleeves. For the first time, I noticed a tiny spider tattoo above his wrist. It was similar to the one on Emily's shoulder.

The first punch knocked me into a leather wing back. I wasn't really seated, more with my crack straddling the arm of the chair. He pulled me up and hit me again and I nearly retched again. The last punch sent me back into the chair—seated this time. My ribs ached and I gasped for air. That's when a call took Zeus' attention away from my beating. He answered the office phone while I doubled over in the chair with my arms crossed, holding my chest.

When he hung up, he pulled rope out of the black duffel and tied me to the chair. "We're not done yet, smartass." With me securely bound, he rolled down his sleeves, put on his jacket, and left the office. This gave me time to get my breathing back to normal. After about ten minutes, the door opened a few inches. I assumed someone was looking in but couldn't see a face. Then it opened quickly, Simone hurried in, turned back towards the hallway and made sure no one was coming. Then she slowly closed the door.

After deciding it was safe, Simone rushed over to my side, "Oh my gosh, are you all right?" She knelt down. "Why are you all the way naked?"

"What do you mean?

"You're all the way naked. When I came in, I thought you were just sort of naked."

"So?"

She looked around. "So, is this 'in trouble' naked, or 'I'm into some weird kink' naked?"

"Look at me. I'm bruised all over the place. Does this look like kink naked?"

She looked me over and thought about it. "Well, you never know. But I guess, given where you are and what you've been dealing with, this is probably in trouble naked." She started to untie me.

"Well, thanks for the vote of confidence. But, don't untie me. Not yet."

She stood back up. "I knew it." She put her hands on her hips. "This is kink naked."

"No, I just think I should be tied up when they get back. Or else they will know someone is here helping me."

"But they're hurting you."

"They won't kill me. They still need me for tomorrow. What about the Temple Cup?"

"Oh, it's in the hallway."

I almost came out of the chair. "You left it out there?"

"It's safe. It's in a food cart, hidden down below."

"Did you look? Did it have the initials? Is it the real one?"

She smiled, looked me up and down, then put both hands on my cheeks. "All in good time." Then she kissed me. "All in good time."

"Don't tease me. Please, I've got to know."

She winked and walked towards the door. Then she opened it quietly, looked both ways and disappeared.

For another ten minutes I was alone, naked, and wondering if Simone could get the Cup safely out of the house. Then my second visitor arrived.

"I've had fantasies about you being tied up and naked," said Emily.

"Really?"

"Yes," she paused and looked around, "but they weren't in this room. And in the dream, you weren't bruised and bleeding."

"Funny, I'm not bleeding in any of my fantasies either."

She asked, "Am I tied up in them?"

"You're assuming my fantasies are about you."

It was at this point that I realized she was holding a bat. It looked like the same bat she had used to smash the baseball decanter the first night I met her. You really shouldn't insult a woman with a bat.

She turned her head slightly and raised the bat with both hands. "Is this the point where you tell me I'm not your type?"

I considered carefully the vulnerable position I was in. And then I lied. Sort of. "You're every man's type."

She took her gaze off the bat, looked at me and smiled. "That's better." Then she moved in close. "Now, tell me about the picture."

"Donnie is going to do it."

She stood up and started to leave. "Good, I'll see you tomorrow."

"Wait, you're just going to leave me here?"

"I'm assuming you're naked and tied up for a reason. Since that reason doesn't involve me or one of *my* fantasies at the moment, I'm going to assume it's none of my business."

Out the door she went, not closing it all the way. When Zeus returned, he asked me why the door was open. "I got hungry and went looking for a sandwich." He slapped me across the face.

"Why is the door open?"

"Because your boss has a bat-shit crazy niece and she came in here to see him I presume."

He pondered that for a while, then untied me. "Get dressed and follow me. You're leaving now."

Whatever had pulled him away earlier had caused him to forget about finishing my beating. I wasn't disappointed. We walked through a series of hallways, and I thought I caught a glimpse of the silver showcase. The light was on inside it.

After a few more turns, he opened a door to the

outside. "Your car's over there," he pointed out the door. "Be on time tomorrow."

As I walked to my car, I noticed the catering staff loading up in the distance. I wondered if Simone had made it out safely. And if so, did she have the Cup? More importantly, was it *the* Cup?

ON AUCTION DAY, normally I would be pumped. But today, I was understandably freaked out and aching from missing tooth to toe. I wouldn't be bidding for me or anyone else. I was there to smile and tell people that everything was legit. Some or most of it was. But even one fake item was a tarnish on the auction and my reputation. Still, I had no choice but to go along.

The event took place in the grand ballroom. But the entire museum was alive with activity. Well-dressed people mingled about, some carrying champagne, some the hastily prepared auction catalog. Museum employees beamed with pride, for this was a unique event. The wealthy and powerful people of Cleveland were here to participate.

Docents told their finest tales of how paintings came to the museum. Board members shuttled wealthy prospects to "must see" collections. The staff was trying to impress the VIPs. The VIPs were trying to impress each other.

I was told to mingle near the baseball items, offer to

answer any questions and assure the skeptics. A man who claimed to be a movie producer inquired about a 19th century scorecard. I think he was offended that I didn't know who he was.

"My last movie starred Matt Damon," he told me.

"Was that the one where he played the gay ventriloquist?" I asked.

He was annoyed. "No, he played Warren Harding." I looked perplexed. "The president," he added.

"Oh, I remember now," I said. "I didn't see it."

"Really?" He seemed disgusted.

"You ever consider making a movie about Taft? That's a movie I would go see. You know he was our fattest president?"

He was about finished with me. "Do you know anything about these scorecards or not?"

"Sure. These were all from the 1895 Temple Cup series. Cleveland won, four games to one over the Baltimore Orioles. Of course, those Orioles are not related to the modern-day franchise. Cleveland had finished second in the National League, but the top two teams faced off in the postseason for the Temple Cup. You could say it was the precursor to the World Series."

"And these were actual scorecards from that series?"

"Yes, sir."

"Thanks," he said and started to walk away.

I called after him, "You know who was president when those games were played? Grover Cleveland!"

He kept walking. "He would make a good movie,

too." He waved me off. "You could even do a sequel. He was president twice, you know. Not in a row!" Apparently, my ideas for presidential feature films don't coincide with those of Hollywood decision makers.

"Grover Cleveland was a misogynistic ass." I turned to see Valerie standing next to me. "Who would want to see a movie about him?"

"Why don't you like Cleveland? Who hates a man named Grover? He's practically a living Muppet."

"He spoke out against women having the right to vote."

"Wow, I had no idea."

"Yeah, well then I'll let it slide. Look, I need to talk to you." She looked around to see who might be listening. "You need to get out of here, Quick."

"I can't. I've got to finish this so I can get these guys off my back."

"Something bad is going to happen here today. I came to warn you because you got the Plank back for me."

"What's going to happen?" Now I was the one looking around. I lowered my voice. "Other than a few people bidding on some fake baseball items."

"Look, you don't want to be here when the auction is over. Duck out when the last item goes up for bidding. Leave the building and don't come back."

"What are you talking about?"

"I can't tell you. Just do it, okay?"

"All right," I assured her. Of course, I was lying. I

didn't plan to leave until I could be sure there were no more documents with my name on them validating some fake memorabilia. And if I was lucky, I wanted to break something over the head of Zeus. Anything.

Before she walked away, I asked, "If it's dangerous, why are you here?"

At that moment, Mr. Bow Tie arrived and put his arm around her shoulder. "We're bidding on one item." She paused, then looked at Stephen. "And then leaving?" She said it almost as a question. He nodded yes to her but said nothing.

"Oh, yeah? What are you bidding on?"

"A portrait of Chief Sockalexis."

The couple left and I pondered this new development. Emily and Valerie were going to bid on the same item? This could get feisty. I wondered if they were selling popcorn.

Before I could find any, I was insulted from behind. "Who dresses you?"

I turned to see Emily and her cousin. She was wearing a blue dress with white polka dots and red heels. Frankie wore jeans, a burgundy tuxedo jacket with no shirt underneath and no socks. "What's wrong with this suit?"

"Well first, you bought it at Macy's." I did. "Second, you bought if off the bargain rack." I did that as well. "And third, you should have had the sleeves altered, they're too long." They were.

"Frankie, when this is over, maybe you can do one of

those makeover deals with me. Then I won't look so hideous."

He seemed enthralled by the idea. "You should be so lucky."

I looked at Emily, "I know why you are here. Why is he here?"

Frankie left us, already bored with the conversation. Emily replied, "He arranged to buy a piece that's on display in the museum that's not part of this auction. It's by an emerging artist named Splatter. Have you heard of him?"

"Of course. I've tasted some of his work." Before the action started, I got the munchies and had gone to the lobby.

"Frankie bought the Lucky Charms Lady Gaga."

"The what?"

"Splatter created a life-sized Lady Gaga statue made completely out of Lucky Charms."

"I'm speechless."

Emily leaned in and whispered, "Is my painting done?"

"Yes, Donnie finished it. But I still don't fully understand what you plan to do with it. If you are going to sell the fake down the road, why did you need it so quickly?"

"I made a deal with Proudfoot to display the painting here in the museum for six months. I plan to display the fake. Then sell it right from here. Nobody will question the authenticity if it's shipped from the museum."

"You really are one of them, aren't you?"

She looked around the room then replied, "No. I'm smarter." She leaned in and gave me a kiss on the cheek. "And naughtier." She leaned back, straightened her skirt, checked herself to make sure everything was perfect, and said, "and infinitely more dangerous."

She left me standing there to contemplate her self-assessment, and the event began. The auction itself was breathtaking—if you're into that sort of thing. I tried to keep score in my head but lost count after it topped $1 million. There were a few random questions about the Spiders and their history, but nobody challenged any of the baseball items or their provenance.

Each of the baseballs I faked sold, which brought approving nods from Tarantola and Newton. As I watched the proceedings, I noticed Emily working her magic on one of the Davis Group employees. He was stationed with all of the jewelry included in the sale. I knew she had to be working some angle for the spider brooch.

Finally, the Chief Sockalexis painting went up for sale. I had suggested a minimum starting bid of $5,000 and that is what the Davis Group went with. Emily quickly raised her bidding paddle. Valerie waited a good twenty seconds to see if anyone else was seriously interested. Then she raised her paddle for $5,500. Emily raised to $6,000 without hesitation.

The game was on. Back and forth, neither looking at the other until Valerie bid $20,000. Emily shot her a wicked glare and took it to $25,000. Valerie jumped to $30,000. Murmurs went throughout the room. I couldn't believe Valerie wanted this painting so badly. Who was her customer?"

Emily bid once more, upping the total by just five hundred dollars. Valerie pounced with $31,000. Going once. Going twice, Sold.

Valerie and Stephen made for the Davis Auction table to settle up. Emily made a direct path to me. "I saw you talking to her before the auction. What are you up to?"

"Me? Why would I want her to win? You don't need the painting Donnie and I supplied you if you don't have the original."

"You're right. I don't. Tell Donnie to keep it."

"Wait, you owe us $10,000 apiece."

She moved in close enough for me to smell her perfume and feel her breath on my neck and cheek. "No $10,000 for you." A little kiss. "No 10,000 for Donnie." Another kiss. And now her body up against me. "And definitely no bonus." I don't know if the last touch was a kiss or a bite. "Goodbye, Quick."

I was basically a zombie for the next two or three auction items. The next thing I can remember, Zeus was ordering me to follow him. From the look of things, there were only half dozen items left to auction. All of them were paintings, so I didn't think much of it. There was no need for my expertise at this point.

"Mr. Tarantola wants to have a word."

I followed him down the hall to the rear loading dock. Donnie was waiting nervously.

"You two wait here. The boss will be along in a minute to settle up."

As soon as he was out of sight, Donnie said, "They're going to kill us."

"I don't think so. I think they're going to tell us we have to keep working for them."

He looked at me skeptically.

"Then if we say no," I added, "they're going to kill us."

He wasn't convinced. "No, they're just going to kill us."

The backup warning beeper of a truck startled both of us. It moved slowly to the edge of the dock. When it stopped, the driver got out, walked around to the back and opened the rear door. He glanced at both of us but didn't say a word. After opening the door, he left us alone.

Zeus returned with a gun drawn. "Into the truck."

"Leaving early?" I asked.

"You are."

Donnie spoke up. "The boss said I was supposed to kill him."

Zeus and I both turned to Donnie and said, "What?"

Donnie ignored me and responded to Zeus. "The

boss told me to stab him to death." He pulled out a knife. "What's the gun for?"

Zeus looked genuinely confused. He stumbled with his words for a moment and Donnie took the opening to stab me in the thigh. As I fell to the ground, I shouted, "What the hell?"

"Yeah, what the hell?" Zeus asked.

Donnie moved in closer and stood over me. "The boss told me to kill him and I'm going to do it. Got a problem with that?"

Zeus sounded unsure. "No, I suppose not."

"Just drag him into the truck farther for me and I'll finish him off."

Zeus obliged. He put his gun in his pocket, bent down, grabbed my arms and pulled me into the truck. With his focus on me, he didn't pay any attention to the man with the knife sliding behind him. Before he had a chance to stand up straight, Donnie stabbed him in the back. Before he could pull the gun out of his pocket, Donnie's next stab pierced his kidney. Zeus wheeled around and Donnie stabbed him once more in the chest.

Donnie watched him breathe his last and then looked at me. "Sorry about your leg, Quick. I had to distract him. The idea just sort of came to me." As quickly as he had killed Zeus, Donnie was tending my wound.

"I need a rag or something to put pressure on your leg."

I looked down and then at Donnie. "I never liked this tie anyway."

He helped me take off my tie, wadded it into a ball, and pressed it on my leg. Then he helped me up out of the truck. He closed the door just in time before the driver came back. When the driver saw blood on the back end of his truck, he cursed.

"No blood, damn it. We had a deal." He grabbed some rags from a nearby pile and did his best to wipe up the crimson mess. Then he tossed the rags at Donnie. "I charge extra for sloppy. Tell the boss this was sloppy. I want ten percent more."

Donnie and I looked at each other and back at the driver. He was here to remove a body all right. Thank God, he didn't have a clue whose body it was supposed to be.

"Repeat it out loud," he shouted at us.

We obliged in unison. "You want 10 percent more because we were sloppy."

"Right. I'll expect the envelope in the usual place by morning."

Off he went, carrying Zeus to wherever I assume they had paid to have Donnie and me buried. Donnie told me to sit and wait on the dock so he could call an ambulance. He also asked me to think up some excuse for how I got injured.

"Don't bother calling an ambulance" I shouted after him.

He yelled back from the hallway. "Why? Don't you want to go to the hospital?"

"Yes, but I don't think the FBI is going to let me leave without making a statement."

"The FBI? What do they have to do with this?"

"Ask them yourself. They're pulling up to the dock."

18

S omber men and women in dark pants and dark sunglasses swarmed the loading dock. Each wore the familiar blue jacket with FBI in yellow across the front and back. The first wave passed right on by me, without a word. Some shouted orders and others began to systematically inspect the merchandise and take pictures.

Donnie abandoned me as soon as he heard me say FBI. He ran back into the museum, but it, too, swarmed with blue jackets. Finally, a familiar looking agent approached me, noticed my wound and called for medical help. Then he spoke.

"Do you remember me, Quick?"

"Now that you mention it, you look like one of the roadies for Shackled Fudge."

"Is that supposed to be funny?"

"It sounded funny in my head. Of course, I've been stabbed so I might not be thinking clearly."

He knelt down. Quietly he said, "I'm Special Agent Griffin. The last time we spoke was in Utah."

It came back to me. Griffin was the FBI agent who brought me to Utah to look at the Sockalexis portrait. He was also the guy I saw talking to Valerie's boyfriend in the hotel and lurking about the lobby of the museum when I discovered the snack food art.

"I remember now. You've been following me around the entire time I've been in Cleveland," I said. "I guess going undercover isn't your strong suit," I added.

"I may have made a few mistakes, but I was pretty sure by the look on your face you hadn't put it together who I was."

"How could you be sure?"

"We're the FBI. We have a very thorough file on you. We know your strengths and your weaknesses."

I didn't like the way he emphasized weaknesses. "And what about my weaknesses made you so sure I didn't remember you?"

"I wasn't wearing a skirt and heels the last time we met."

I nodded in agreement. "That is a very thorough file."

"You know, when that portrait went missing, I always thought you had something to do with it."

"Funny," I replied. "When I saw it in the Tarantola collection, I thought you sold it to them."

He laughed, "I guess we both had the wrong guy. But I'm not here about the painting. I've come to make you a deal."

This caught me off guard. "What?"

"We're going to get you out of here now, get you to the hospital and patched up."

"And what do I have to do?"

"I wasn't finished. As far as the people we're arresting today know, you ducked out early. Donnie is going to admit to killing Zeus in self-defense. We've got him muzzled and we'll make him an offer shortly."

"But I was with Donnie when it happened."

"That's part of his deal. He will say you were long gone when he and Zeus fought. Same with the driver of the truck. He's been detained about two blocks from here."

"Why?"

"Because we don't want anyone in Satellite to know you're working for us."

"I'm not working for you."

"Even though I'm pretty sure you were coerced into working with Tarantola and Newton, you were still doing things that were illegal, correct?"

"Maybe I should talk to my lawyer before I answer that."

"There won't be any need for that, if you help us out. Look Quick, I'm not blackmailing you. Well, I am, kind of. I'm offering you a job."

"Doing what?"

"We've been investigating art fraud by Tarantola and his partners for a while now."

"But what does that have to do with me?"

"Newton approached him and offered to team up. Satellite was already creating memorabilia fakes, and Newton saw the opportunity to expand into art."

"I'm not following you."

"To make a long story short, we're going to charge Tarantola with art forgery and crimes related to that. We're leaving the memorabilia fraud network intact."

"Why?"

"So, you can help us catch Satellite."

"Does that job come with hazard pay?" I asked.

"You will be compensated for your time and effort," he said.

"Won't Tarantola blab about Newton and Satellite?"

"You saw the picture of Archie."

"Fair enough," I replied.

"I would like you to help us bring down the whole thing."

"I'll think about it," I answered.

I was mulling over his offer while a couple of EMTs worked on me. The back of the ambulance door opened, and Special Agent Griffin stepped inside. "There's one witness that we're not sure about, and we'd like for you to listen in on the interrogation. One of us will accompany you to the hospital, then bring you to our office after you're released. Any questions?"

One of the EMTs interjected, "The hospital is going to want to keep him overnight. He's lost a lot of blood."

"I just need him for a few hours. You can have him back when we're done."

The EMT looked at me. I shrugged. "I don't think I have any choice."

Special Agent Griffin responded, "No, he doesn't." He opened the door and called for someone named Martinez. I could hear him speaking to her but couldn't hear the instructions.

Special Agent Martinez climbed into the ambulance. She was stunning, with long dark brown hair and matching eyes. She smiled and said she'd follow the ambulance and wait for the ER to stabilize me.

Martinez's smile warmed me to the idea of working for the FBI. After she stepped out of the ambulance, I closed my eyes and pictured her warm brown eyes and that cascade of brown curls. When we got to the hospital, she was nowhere to be found. I was expecting some sort of hand holding (literally) while they gave me shots, cleaned my wound, and stitched me up. The emergency room doctor insisted I be attached to an IV for an hour and there was still no sign of the fetching special agent.

But as soon as the IV bag was empty and the doctor told me I was free to go, Martinez pushed a wheelchair into the room and helped me out of the bed. I was still in my hospital gown. "Shouldn't I have pants?"

"I'm just going to bring you right back."

"But I'm in a hospital gown. I look ridiculous!"

"Take a blanket with you?"

"That's stealing," I said. "You should know better, you're in the FBI."

"We're coming right back, I promise."

I grabbed the blanket off the bed and covered myself as best I could.

"I look ridiculous."

"You said that already."

As she helped me get into her car, I caught a good whiff of her perfume. I was sort of smitten. Maybe it was the painkillers.

When we got to the FBI office, Martinez helped me out of the car and into the wheelchair. She still smelled nice. After taking me inside, we took an elevator to the second floor. On the way to the interrogation rooms, I noticed Valerie and her boyfriend Stephen speaking to a special agent in a conference room. They didn't see me.

Griffin met us and opened the door for Martinez to push me into an observation room. Through a large one-way mirror, I could see Emily Tarantola wearing the same dress she wore at the auction. But now, pinned to her upper right chest, was the spider brooch.

The agent in the room with Emily asked her question after question about the art forgery. She pleaded ignorance each time. And each time Special Agent Griffin asked me if she was telling the truth. I was torn. I was wildly attracted to her, yet I knew she was capable of as much evil as her uncle. As I weighed all the events of the past few weeks, I couldn't recall a single one that connected her to the scam. Even when I was tied up in her uncle's office the night before, she had said it was none of her business.

"Do you believe her?" Martinez asked.

"I can't think of one thing that she said or did over the last couple of weeks that could implicate her in her uncle's dealings."

"I find it hard to believe she's innocent."

"She's anything but innocent," I replied. Some sixth sense in her must have heard that, because Emily turned towards the mirror and gave just the slightest wicked smirk. "But I can't think of anything she said that would prove she knew about the forgeries."

"She knew about Donnie."

"Yes, but that doesn't prove she knew exactly what he was hired to do for her uncle. Look, if she's guilty, I'm all for sending her to jail. But I just can't say with any certainty she was part of the plan."

In my mind, the proof that Emily wasn't part of it was pinned to her chest. It seemed to me that her fight to keep the brooch and her desire to buy back the Sockalexis painting were at cross purposes with her uncle's plans with Satellite. Her plan to have Donnie forge paintings for her told me she was a chip off the old block, just not involved with the family's illicit business. She was branching out on her own.

But do I tell all of this to Griffin? Or do I just let it

play out? I watched Emily as the special agent continued to question her. "Why doesn't she have an attorney with her?" I asked.

"She said she didn't need or want one," Griffin answered.

And she didn't. The more the special agent talked, the more he became tangled in her web. She played with her hair. She leaned in and touched his hand a few times. Then she would sit back and cross her legs. Each subsequent question became less direct, less challenging. Each answer less on topic. Another fifteen minutes and they were talking about their favorite sushi restaurant and what a coincidence it was that they both loved the same one. I doubted she had actually ever set foot in the place. Griffin even muttered, "I love that restaurant."

I looked at Special Agent Martinez and she rolled her eyes. I asked, "Can we go now?"

Griffin gave the okay for me to go and she wheeled me out of the room. On the way, we ran into Valerie and Stephen. "Thanks for the heads-up," I said, looking down at my leg. "I almost got out in time." I looked directly at Valerie. "How did you know?"

She looked at Stephen and asked, "It's okay to share now, right?" He nodded. "Stephen was helping the FBI. He inquired about several of the forged paintings and bid on them. They've been investigating these guys for a year now and Stephen has been buying fake paintings for the FBI. With his help," she squeezed his hand, "it looks like they have a pretty solid case."

I turned to him, "You're a hell of a citizen."

"I hope you're not in too much trouble for your part in all of this, 'just Quick.' "

"Don't you worry your pretty little head, Stephen. I'm going to be just fine." I looked at Valerie, "You kids stay out of trouble now."

Martinez took me back to the hospital. I tried to small talk with her along the way, but she wasn't much for chatting. Something about Emily's performance had left her irritated with all men. Since I was the man in closest proximity, I took her disdain for the team. She brought me back to the same room and watched while the nurse helped me into bed.

"Thanks for your help," I said. "Will I see you again?"

"Not likely. I don't think the job they have in mind for you is in Cleveland."

"Where is it?"

"Not for me to say," she said. "Good luck, Quick."

I slept long and hard and didn't wake until the next morning. After I ate a gourmet breakfast of toast spread with what passed for butter and eggs that tasted like plastic, Griffin dropped by.

"How are you feeling?"

"Better until each time the pain meds wear off. Good enough to go home today, I hope."

"Have you thought about our offer?"

"Did Donnie agree?"

"Without hesitating."

"So, he's off the hook?"

"No, he'll do a little time for the forgery, but we'll see that he is put in a minimum-security facility and out on parole quickly."

"I don't understand."

"He has too many priors for him not to get some time. If we put him out on the street immediately it would be like tattooing 'informant' on his forehead."

"I really don't have a choice, do I?"

"Not really. If you say no, then you've got both us and Satellite to worry about. They'd likely be looking to retaliate. With our offer, they still think you're useful to them, and thus useful to us."

"Lucky me. What about Emily?"

"Nothing in our year-long investigation tied her to the art forgery scam. And nothing in the past few weeks with your involvement changed that for us. So, for now, we're not pursuing her."

"Good for her, I guess."

"She did ask for one of the paintings back. Said it was a family heirloom that shouldn't have been part of the auction."

"Did you give it to her?"

"She was very convincing."

"You didn't fall for it, did you?"

"I've interviewed a lot of beautiful women in my career. I'm not that easy to seduce."

"I wasn't so sure yesterday."

"She may have gotten to Special Agent Hook, but I held my ground when I interrogated her."

"So, what about the painting?"

"I figured you would have something to say about it, since it's a portrait of a ballplayer."

"It belongs to a Native American tribe on the east coast," I said. "Not sitting in some evidence locker for the next few years while this thing plays out in court."

"This could be the first act of trust between us in this new partnership. What if someone were to make an anonymous donation? Would that convince you?"

"Maybe. I still need some time to think it over."

"Call me when you're ready?" He extended his hand and I shook it.

I DIDN'T GET PAID for any of the work I did for Newton, Tarantola or his goons the past few weeks. So, I didn't feel even slightly guilty for keeping the large trophy that sat before me on my kitchen table. I hadn't looked inside yet, and Simone, if she had, wasn't telling me. She sat beside me and held my hand.

Through all this trauma, I had come to really like Simone. She was quirky and weird and probably on the road to becoming a lifetime criminal. It probably wouldn't work out. She was also sexy, intensely loyal and resourceful. It would probably be fun while it lasted.

"Are you nervous?"

"Yes, a little bit," I answered.

I had spent an extra day in Cleveland after getting out of the hospital. Simone came to get me and drove me back. We left at 4 a.m. because I was still paranoid that Satellite was watching me, and I didn't want Simone to be involved. But now we were sitting together back in my home, about to find out if we had a fortune in front of us.

I stood up and tilted it towards me, inspecting the inner rim of the trophy. I rotated it and felt with my hands as well, in case the initials were too small or worn to see. As my hand moved across it, I felt something rough. Rotating that point into the light, I saw the "D" and the "N." This wasn't *a* Temple Cup. It was *the* Temple Cup. The one in the Baseball Hall of Fame was a copy.

I sat back down and looked at Simone.

"It's the real thing, isn't it?"

"Yes, it is."

"How much do you think we can get?"

I thought about a price. I wasn't going to have the conflict with this piece like I did the Wagner card. I wanted to turn this one over fast. "Conservatively, I would say a half million to $750,000."

She squealed. "That is so sexy!"

Then she kissed me hard and slid onto my lap. My turn to squeal. "My leg."

"Sorry, sorry, sorry," she said and got off me gently as possible.

I looked her in the eyes and said, "Thank you for taking such a risk for me."

She kissed me again. "It was my pleasure. Now, let's sell that bad boy!"

I called Dr. Walsh and let him know I had an item he could earn a little commission on. When I told him what it was, he was beside himself.

"You found the real Temple Cup? How?"

"You really should not ask those kinds of questions," I answered. "Do you think your friend will be interested?"

"Absolutely. How much are we talking?"

"I think it would get between $500,000 to $700,000 at auction. But I will let him have it for $450,000 if he can pay right away and keep this discreet."

The possibility of this item being illicit made my dentist even more excited. "Discreet, huh. I'll call him right now. And I get a cut?"

"And you get a cut."

"Quick, you're the best. Talk with you soon."

On Saturday, Simone drove me to meet Kevin at Beagle's Safes and Security on the east side of Indianapolis. This was the company he had found to open my safe. Simone was giddy. Kevin was cranky. I was sick to my stomach. When I get near a truly valuable artifact, I have a sixth sense about it. Like when I was drawn to the silver showcase in the Tarantola house. But now, I felt nothing.

"I'm Frank Beagle. Are you Mr. Quick?"

"I am. Nice to meet you."

"Pleasure to serve you. Let's have a look at your safe."

Kevin placed it on a workbench and Beagle inspected it. "Uh-huh, Uh-huh," he hummed over and over as he looked at it.

"Are there any valuables in it now?"

"Yes, something worth a lot of money."

"Uh-huh. I can get it open. I'll be gentle, too. Give me about twenty minutes."

He offered us all seats and we watched as he went to work with various tools. I could pretend I knew what he used, but why lie to you? Tools are not my thing. If you need to fix a car, I'm not your guy. But authenticate that 19th century baseball program in your granddad's attic, I'm your guy.

Almost exactly twenty minutes later he announced, "And here we go."

It popped open. I stood to look inside. The Honus Wagner card was gone. In its place was a white business card with the Satellite logo on it. I picked it up and turned it over, but it was blank.

Kevin let out a string of expletives.

Simone squeezed my hand and tried to console me. "At least we still have the Cup."

I nodded without responding out loud. Kevin, Mr. Beagle, and Simone were all talking at once, but I had tuned everything out and just stared at the empty safe. Finally, I realized everything was silent and they were staring at me.

"Mr. Beagle, thank you for getting it open." I handed him my credit card then pulled out my phone as he went to process my payment.

Scrolling through my contacts, I found the name I was looking for and dialed. When he gave me his business card, I had meant to throw it away. And I did, but for some reason I saved the number on my phone. I swore I wouldn't use it. But you never get out of the web.

"This is Special Agent Griffin speaking."

"It's Quick. How soon can I start?"

ABOUT THE AUTHOR

Jeff Stanger writes funny novels that usually have the game of baseball as a backdrop. You don't have to be a student of the game or even a fan to enjoy them, however. There is enough mystery, danger, and even romance to keep you on the edge of your seat. His current work includes the Quick Baseball Mystery Series which follows the exploits of a rare baseball memorabilia dealer who always seems to land himself in the middle of a criminal case to be solved.

The first installment, *The Fungo Society*, finds Quick at Spring Training trying to find a rare game-used jersey. Along the way, he meets a group of old ballplayers named the Fungo Society. Think Bull Durham meets Grumpy Old Men meets Oceans 11! *The Fungo Society* was Shelf Unbound's Runner-Up for Best Indie Book of the Year.

In addition, Stanger has written *Trolley Dodgers* which follows the Midwest college town of Bloomington, IN as they try to buy the Los Angeles Dodgers. He also wrote *Kansaska*, a funny look back at the semi-pro minor leagues of the 1940s.

Stanger lives and writes in Carmel, Indiana.

ALSO BY JEFF STANGER

Quick Mysteries

The Fungo Society

72 Hours in Savanah

Other Novels

Trolley Dodgers

Kansaska

www.ingramcontent.com/pod-product-compliance
Lightning Source LLC
Chambersburg PA
CBHW070636170726
48291CB00003B/1039